LAST RESORT

Other books by Rebecca L. Boschee:

Mulligan Girl

LAST RESORT

•

Rebecca L. Boschee

AVALON BOOKS
NEW YORK

Published by Avalon Books,
an imprint of Thomas Bouregy & Co., Inc.
160 Madison Avenue, New York, NY 10016

Library of Congress Cataloging-in-Publication Data

Boschee, Rebecca L.
    Last resort / Rebecca Boschee.
        p. cm.
    ISBN 978-0-8034-7659-2
    I. Title.
    PS3602.O833L37 2011
    813'.6—dc22
                        2010046209

PRINTED IN THE UNITED STATES OF AMERICA
ON ACID-FREE PAPER
BY RR DONNELLEY, BLOOMSBURG, PENNSYLVANIA

For my family:
thank you for giving me the courage
to dive headfirst into my dreams.

Chapter One

NOW IS THE TIME FOR A NEW OUTLOOK;
LOOK OUT.
LUCKY NUMBERS: 3 5 24 36 28 11

Jackson glanced around the empty office before stepping out and slamming the door behind him. He turned to face the reception and gathering area for his father's business. *Funny, I still think of it as my father's business.* Less than three weeks ago it had been a haven to lounge in and chat up vacationers between tours. Now it served as an aching reminder. *My own unbelievably successful albatross.* Jackson's nostrils flared, taking in salt air as he advanced toward the door leading outside. With a surge of relief, he realized that despite the sweltering humidity, it became easier to breathe the nearer he came to the exit. Yes, this was the right thing to do. This was what he needed. He had no doubt Cast-a-Line Charters and Tours would be here when he got back. Heck, it'd probably flourish while he was away.

A woman with cropped bronze hair leaped off a stool near the counter and laid her tanned hand on his shoulder. She contemplated him with sympathetic eyes. The weight, akin to a three-hundred-pound loggerhead, may have been crushing Jackson's chest, but the sight of Emmalee Caruthers stretched up on her toes to comfort him made the corners of his lips twitch. He knew his behavior over the past weeks since his father's death distressed her. She'd made it clear she considered

1

his decision to pack up his life on Tybee Island and make tracks for Florida a grave mistake, but he needed a diversion, and that was what had presented itself.

"Jacky," Emmalee said. "We can't help you if you run away."

Jackson sucked in a breath, letting it out before responding. He'd already been through this once with Manny, the skiff captain who took pods of vacationers or nature enthusiasts to the inland marshes for fishing and sightseeing. Manny had broken his characteristic silence to grill Jackson about his decision. Now Emmalee wasn't going to let him pass without voicing her qualms.

Jackson ran calloused fingers through his hair, not caring if the longer strands stood on end. *Geez.* It wasn't like he'd renounced his inheritance and abandoned the business. He and his father had toiled too long over the past nine years building it. Even when Jackson had gone off to college, he'd come back most weekends, summers, and holidays to do what he did best. After graduating magna cum laude, he'd nailed his diploma into a wall stud beside a photo of his mother and taken over the books along with his regular water duties. That freed his father to advance from dreaming about expanding their business to planning it. Jackson pondered his father's obsession with building another small tour company in either Puerto Rico or Mexico, and he felt his jaw muscle working. No, Jackson thought, he didn't want to give up his father's dreams forever. He just needed to get away.

"It's not like I'm running off to join the circus, Pug." Jackson shifted the knapsack over his shoulder and narrowed his eyes at the childhood friend he'd known for twenty-three years. She could irritate him like fresh water on a jellyfish sting, but she was the closest thing he had to a sibling.

"You may as well be, Jacky. Selling out to work at a resort, and an all-inclusive one at that. Your mama'll be rolling in the grave."

Her hand flew off his shoulder and cupped her mouth as she realized the probable insensitivity of what she'd said. Pug didn't possess large quantities of tact. She pretty much spoke her mind. Fortunately, the wound left by the loss of Jackson's mother had dulled long ago. His father's recent stroke was a different matter. Jackson felt painfully aware he should've been with him, marlin fishing on the sound that day. Had he not been sweet-talking one of the island's local beauties into a picnic on the pier, he would've been. Logic told him it wouldn't have changed the outcome, but at least Jackson would have been with his father. At least he'd have been able to say good-bye.

He pulled Pug's hand away from her face and gave it a squeeze.

She examined him through squinted eyes. "Is this something you have to do?"

Jackson nodded. "I'll be back outside of six months, nine at most. And I'll keep in touch, of course. I've got access to the Internet to download the books and keep an eye on things. Not that I need to. You and Manny could run this place with your eyes closed."

"Not without the Kobles." Pug dropped her gaze to the floor.

Jackson placed a finger under her chin and raised her face. "I'm coming back when I figure things out. Promise."

"Don't take too long." Her eyes misted for a moment before a glimmer shot into them. "You play nice with those midwestern girls who are always traipsing down to Florida on vacation. I know what a heartbreaker you can be. I've seen the aftermath."

Jackson gave a low snort.

"I'm not kidding. Those poor gals from Indiana nearly threw themselves overboard when you didn't pay them the right kind of attention."

"You and I have been around long enough to know to avoid that kind of relationship with paying customers. Besides, I can't risk falling for someone. People I love tend to leave for good." Jackson forced a light tone, but he felt the tightness around his heart, and he knew Pug could probably read it in his eyes. The damn loggerhead just put on a few pounds.

Pug looked tempted to throw her arms around him. She opted for their routine humor instead. "I'm not talking about *love,* Jackson Koble. What about the divas working for that monstrosity you're flitting off to? You know they'll be dying for a big ol' helping of Southern hospitality. Don't try telling me you can always resist *them*."

Jackson gave her a sly smile. "*Those* young ladies know perfectly well what they're getting into, and so do I."

Pug snorted, but she reached up and gave him a peck on the cheek, blinking too fast. "Don't hide away forever. Come home soon."

"I'll miss you too, Pug." He patted the top of her head and stepped outside into the sunshine.

It didn't seem right that the sky off the coast could be so bright while his whole world caved in. Jackson squinted at a sea bird soaring overhead. No, he wasn't deserting the business. He just needed to figure out what to do next.

Chapter Two

WHEN A DOOR CLOSES, A WINDOW OPENS;
WATCH OUT FOR WHAT THE DRAFT BLOWS IN.
LUCKY NUMBERS: 44 2 14 39 26 12

The vase Lila hurled at the door clunked to the floor in pieces. *Like what's left of my plans.* She pictured Brody's expression behind his trademark aviator sunglasses. Unfortunately, he'd realized her intent in time to dodge the crockery, depriving her of justice. She retreated to the bathroom and squeezed her lips shut, biting back the wave of nausea.

The lowlife snake had cheated. He'd cheated and hadn't even tried to deny it. Instead, he'd had the audacity to assume she'd take him back after a pitiful apology. He hadn't even looked sorry. Lila dropped her head in her hands. Not only had she lost a boyfriend, albeit a pathetic one, she'd lost the three thousand dollars for next semester's tuition. A sensitive person might've been more concerned about the loss of love, but the fury consuming Lila wouldn't allow it.

Why did I lend him money? For a ski trip, of all things! She'd never have agreed if she'd realized he would quit his job and use the remnant of her tuition money to snuggle up to some dumb snow bunny. Lila raised her head to stare at the reflection in the mirror, surprised by how pallid her face looked. Even her year-round Arizona suntan didn't help. *Well, who wouldn't look sickly after hearing the man she'd wasted ten months on had snowed her?*

5

Brody excelled at sensitivity and charm. He had laid it on thick with Lila. Suave and attentive, he'd made her feel like the center of the universe. She should have realized that kind of talent came from lots of practice. When he'd turned off the charm after they agreed to be exclusive, she assumed it was because she'd been too reclusive, spending too much time on her schoolwork and writing. In the past months, she'd made an effort to pay him more attention. Now she could see he'd taken advantage of her.

Her cheeks burned. *At least now I have some color in my face.* Lila switched on the faucet and splashed lukewarm water on her face. She wasn't going to waste another moment mourning a guy who couldn't *spell* the word commitment, let alone practice it. She had bigger things to worry about now, like paying for rent and spring semester tuition. She'd have to call Cliff to finagle extra work before school started.

Writing training materials full time for the Scottsdale office of Tour Paradise, Inc. may not have been the glamorous writing career Lila dreamt of, but it paid the bills. After two years of saving, it had helped her go to college. Now, with two semesters left before graduating with a major in English, she worked part time for Cliff. When her nose wasn't buried in a book, she kept a diary. Writing was great therapy. Even now, as she prickled over her current situation, she could appreciate how the experience would provide fodder for her journal.

She calculated what would happen if Cliff wouldn't let her pick up extra hours. Her mind flicked past her options and flitted instead to what she knew she couldn't do. She couldn't waitress—she was too uncoordinated. She couldn't bartend—watching guys like Brody in action would be a constant irritation. She couldn't move back in with her parents or ask them for money—that, especially, couldn't be done. Her parents would understand, but they'd instilled in her a resourcefulness that didn't include crawling home at the ripe age of twenty-four. She would find another way.

"Fired?" Lila asked, incredulous.

"Not fired, Lila . . . downsized. I'm sorry it's come to this." Dark circles shadowed Cliff's eyes. He ran one hand through thinning hair and cast his gaze between Lila and her co-worker Gina, somehow managing not to look either in the eye.

"But . . . why *us?*" Gina asked.

"It's not just the training department, ladies. I have to downsize a third of the sales force. This has been a long time coming." He spread his hands in front of him. "Regional sales are dismal. The phones aren't ringing. We counted on peak season to compensate, but we're nowhere near last year's numbers. Leisure travel has been hit hard by the downturn in the economy."

Gina stared past him outside his window, a numb look on her face. Lila covered Gina's hand with her own and squeezed it while trying to absorb Cliff's explanation.

"I realize it's unconventional not to tell each of you in private, but we're like a family here, and there's another possibility I wanted to discuss together." Cliff hesitated.

Lila's panic ebbed a little.

"I'm open to possibilities," Gina said before Lila could voice the same thought. Of course Gina would be open to anything Cliff had to offer. She had three young kids and an unemployed ex-husband to consider.

"I can afford to keep both of you part time, or . . . one of you full time. I don't like putting you on the spot with that choice, but I'm fairly sure if the Asian sector does well this season, I can hire you both back full time in the spring."

Lila's hopes plummeted. She couldn't support herself until spring on a part-time salary. If she couldn't do it, there's no way Gina could.

Gina was already shaking her head.

Cliff picked up a stress ball and squeezed. "Are you sure, Gina? Think it through, because if part time won't work, I have to make a choice to keep only one of you. If I do that, I have to look at business results to guide me." His eyes met Lila's.

Lila's stomach dropped. She had earned the top performance review last year, whereas Gina had struggled to meet expectations because of absenteeism. Not her fault. Two of her kids had caught pneumonia.

"No chance. I can't make rent on half my income," Gina said.

Cliff shook his head. "I'm sorry to hear that. I'm afraid—"

"I volunteer," Lila said.

Cliff gawked at her. "You *volunteer* to be laid off?"

Lila pressed her lips together and nodded so she wouldn't change her mind. If Gina lost her job, there'd be more at stake than a delayed graduation.

Gina chewed her bottom lip. "I can't let you do that, Lila."

Her expression was so hopeful Lila almost laughed. "Too late. It's already settled." Lila may not have anyone to rely on, but at least no one else relied directly on her. She knew her reputation for being stubborn would prevent an argument. Not that she expected one.

Tears welled in Gina's eyes, and she leapt up to give Lila a hug. "Lila, you're the best. If there's ever anything I can do for you . . ."

Lila returned the hug and tried not to think of her shattered plans. "Just keep those kids healthy."

When Gina left, Cliff sank in his chair and leaned across the desk with his fingers steepled. He stared at Lila a long time before speaking. "You're really something, Lila. If I can't keep you, it'd be great to keep you with the company. Would you be open to working on locale?"

On locale meant working at one of the resorts, not behind the scenes in an office. If she was on location she couldn't be enrolled in school. But then, if she didn't have any money, she couldn't be enrolled in school, either.

"There's a position open with the kids program, Little Delights, at the resort in Florida. Have you worked with kids before?"

Lila stared past him, an idea forming. Maybe she could take the rest of the semester to work on locale, then make up the missed credits at summer school. She typically took summers off, so what difference would it make if she took a break during spring semester instead? If she could get someone to sublet her apartment, she could save most of her paycheck . . . Tour Paradise paid room and board for resort employees. She could make it work. The idea of putting six states between her and Brody was incentive too.

"Babysitting? A younger brother or sister perhaps?"

Lila straightened in her chair. "No siblings to speak of, but I did work at a summer camp when I was a teenager." *No need to mention it was as an aide in the kitchen.* "And I'm CPR certified."

"Well, that's something. The offer is yours if you want to think about it."

Lila bit her bottom lip. Working at the resort would be way outside her comfort zone. While she was friendly, she wasn't outgoing, and no one would call her bubbly. Still, she could do anything for a few months. She gave Cliff her sunniest, most confident smile. "No need. When do I start?"

Chapter Three

YOU'LL SOON BE KNEE-DEEP IN EXCITING ADVENTURE;
DON'T FORGET TO BRING A SHOVEL.
LUCKY NUMBERS: 18 3 46 2 31 22

Jackson propped his elbows on the back of the bench and let his head fall back for a full view of the stars. A palm frond flapped in the breeze, intermittently blocking the view. He shifted in his seat and inhaled the scent of orange blossoms. In spite of the peaceful surroundings, he hated working arrivals and departures. He couldn't understand why everyone, regardless of job title, was required to participate in the rotation of the mundane duties around the resort. At this hour, when arrival traffic was almost nonexistent, he found it especially difficult. There was nothing to distract his mind from wandering to places he didn't want it to go.

He slid a look at the Italian woman sitting on the bench next to him. Her white shorts were cut high to reveal long legs, which she rubbed as they waited for the next arrival. *Well, almost nothing.* True, he'd long ago decided Isabelle packed too much drama to get involved with, but he couldn't deny that she was stunning.

"Someone is here!" She jumped up and strode toward the headlights that illuminated the drop-off area.

Jackson righted himself and followed. Isabelle loved to talk, so all he'd have to do is carry luggage. He glanced at his watch. In another half-hour he'd call it a night. He wanted to get online to review Cast-a-Line's quarterly earnings to determine how much cash would be available for expansion—not that he'd made any formal decisions to expand just yet. As he thought of the business responsibilities he'd inherited, he felt renewed appreciation for his temporary escape.

Isabelle was at the curb and had engaged the newcomer in small talk. Jackson jogged to catch up.

"Welcome to Encantadora! This is your first time to Florida?" Isabelle flashed a practiced smile.

Jackson found himself transfixed, not by Isabelle's smile, but by the woman standing opposite her in conversation.

"Um, no. I used to come here with my family." A good two inches taller than Isabelle, the woman had pouty lips and troubled brown eyes, eyes a man could get lost in if he wasn't careful. She looked too serious to be on vacation. He scanned the cab. No travel companion, boyfriend, husband, or child accompanied her. People rarely traveled to Encantadora alone. She had to be either a new staff member or a company executive, and she didn't display the arrogance of the latter.

The woman chewed a fingernail on her left hand as she responded to Isabelle's questions. She caught Jackson's eye and started, averting her eyes before following Isabelle away from the curb.

That was unexpected. He'd gotten some strange reactions from girls around the resort, most of which involved overt visual groping, but he'd never evoked panic before. She hadn't even tried to ask them any questions. Most newcomers were so giddy to be embarking on their dream jobs they bombarded whoever worked arrivals with questions about resort life. Intrigued, Jackson lifted the luggage from the curb and followed the women at a short distance.

"It's your first time at Encantadora?" Isabelle asked.

"Yes," the woman responded. "But I'm not—"

"First time at a Tour Paradise resort?"

"No, and I'm not—"

"You will like us here." Isabelle strode toward the pink-and-white open-air building that housed reception. "We make for a comfortable vacation."

"Yes, I know."

"After you check in, I'll show you to your room." She indicated the long counter in a lobby filled with vibrant potted plants and slow-moving rattan ceiling fans. Bougainvillea crept up the white pillars framing the area and cascaded across a latticework ceiling.

Jackson noticed the woman still had her mouth open, presumably to correct some misunderstanding with Isabelle, but she snapped it closed when the receptionist behind the counter rendered her a hostile look.

Jenna. Jenna had a ready dose of jealousy for anyone who might present the slightest competition. This particular woman had the double misfortune of arriving during one of Jackson's shifts. Jenna had made it clear she had designs on Jackson. She thought him rebellious because of his good-natured refusal to conform to some of the more ludicrous of the resort's requirements. Tustin, the general manager, had been tolerant of Jackson as long as he continued his stellar performances on the river where it counted. That, he never failed to do. Impressing girls like Jenna came as an unintended and unwelcome consequence as far as Jackson was concerned. Her small-minded jealously proved an outright nuisance.

"No need to wait around for her, Isabelle; she's not a guest." Jenna said.

"Oh!" Isabelle searched Lila for confirmation.

"It's true. My name is Lila Hayes." Lila's eyes were apologetic. "I'm from the Scottsdale office. I'm here to work on locale for a few months." She swept a lock of chestnut hair away from her face and tucked it behind one ear.

A nervous habit, Jackson guessed by the way she repeated the gesture even after the strand was clear. He watched her with mounting interest. She was pretty enough to work at the resort, but she seemed reserved. She also had a sort of detached absentmindedness about her, like she didn't want to be here. If she didn't want to be at Encantadora, why was she here?

"Well, then, I welcome you to our family." Isabelle recovered from the brief surprise. "I am sure we will be good friends."

She gave a little wave and sauntered back toward the bench. Jackson had no intention of leaving just yet. He dropped the luggage and leaned against a pillar, crossing his arms over his chest.

"Travel documents, please," Jenna said.

Lila rummaged through her shoulder bag. "I'm sure they're here in my purse somewhere."

Jenna responded with a silent glare.

Jackson felt a pang of protectiveness, which didn't pass, even when he realized Lila hadn't noticed Jenna's sour look.

Lila surfaced with the documents and Jenna took the packet with exaggerated impatience, tapping her keyboard. Lila looked perplexed by Jenna's demeanor, but not intimidated. Jenna looked up from her screen and handed Lila a plastic room key, a map, and a paper printout.

"You'll be in Room 303 tonight, a guest room. Don't get comfortable, because you'll move in with the rest of your roommates by five o'clock tomorrow . . . That'll be Room 209. Follow the schedule for the week." Jenna tapped a pen against the printout. "Don't try to be creative. Just wear the colors indicated and don't be late reporting to Little Delights. Try to remember this isn't *your* vacation."

Lila concentrated on the paper in front of her. Jackson noticed her hands shook. He straightened away from the pillar, cursing Jenna for her rudeness and on the brink of making it verbal.

"You managed to avoid the rotations this week," Jenna continued. "By next week, you'll pull duty in the shows, arrivals, and departures, and at the nightclub—so don't get used to the cushy schedule."

Even from his distance, Jackson could see the schedule was packed with activities.

"Cushy, right. Thanks." Lila bit her bottom lip until it turned white.

Jackson stepped forward to intervene until he realized Lila shook from suppressed laughter, not Jenna's bullying. He leaned back against the pillar and smiled. The girl had an interesting sense of humor.

Lila turned away from Jenna, her mouth curved into a smile as she started toward her luggage. Jackson emerged from the shadows. She reached out to clutch one of the bags at the same time he latched on to the handle. Their fingers grazed. An abrupt thunderbolt of energy flared from the point of contact, up Jackson's arm and straight through him. Everything inside him constricted. He blinked at Lila, stunned.

Lila pulled her hand back with uncommon speed. She tucked it under her arm and clamped down, trying to steady her breathing. She hadn't expected anyone to be waiting for her. Why hadn't he gone off with the Italian girl?

She raised her eyes to meet the man who'd sent what felt like a few hundred kilowatts of electricity pulsing through her body. Even though Lila stood five-foot-nine, she had to look up to see into his face. The line of his jaw and angles of his face appeared more rugged and handsome than she'd thought from a distance, as if he spent a great deal of time outdoors. Still, something in his expression impressed her as being almost soft.

She wondered why he wasn't dressed in turquoise and white, like the others. In fact, he looked out of uniform in flip-flops, tan cargo shorts, and a faded T-shirt advertising some island crab shack. She peeked at his fingers, still curled around the handle of her bag. His hands, strong and tanned, were clearly accustomed to hard work. Her mind flitted to an image of what those fingers might feel like caressing her skin. She winced, annoyed. It'd been a long day. She shouldn't be thinking about this man's physical appearance, let alone the rush she'd imagined when they'd touched. Hadn't she promised herself she was done with good-looking men forever? She eyed the man with determination.

Assessing green eyes returned the gaze. Lila felt her heart stammer, and she had to breathe through her nose to control it. A whiff of something sweet drifted in on the night air. Gardenias, maybe.

"Really, you don't have to . . ." Lila started to protest.

Before her eyes, the man melted from stiff curiosity to the picture of relaxation. The effect was like watching a wave wash over a sand castle and soften all the packed edges.

"You think you can haul both these bags across two acres and up three flights of stairs in the dark?" His voice was playful and challenging.

Lila willed herself not to notice the charming Southern lilt accenting his words. She tried to focus on his obvious flaws, like . . . well . . . he *did* seem pretty cocky. "What, you don't have elevators?" she said.

The edge of the man's lip curled upward, and a teasing glint darted into his eyes.

Lila's stomach flipped over. She gritted her teeth in protest.

"They're for guests only."

"Oh." Lila felt her face fall as she contemplated the enormity of the two bags into which she'd packed practically every outfit and pair of shoes she owned.

She made it a point to avoid Jackson's eyes. She couldn't afford to let her defenses down, not in this place, not with this guy. *This* guy definitely fell into the category of too-good-looking-for-his-own-good.

The man watched as she felt a portion of her internal battle play across her face. "Don't worry, Miss . . ."

"Lila."

"Lila, from Scottsdale." He gave her a lazy smile.

He'd heard that?

"I'm Jackson."

Of course. Why couldn't he be Bernie or Felix?

"I won't let you strain yourself. Never say I'm not a gentle-man. You can take the one with the wheels." He headed toward a dimly lit walkway lined with fan palms. Lila didn't follow right away. She could see the path veered toward the low build-ings farthest from the bright lights and sounds at the resort's center.

"Better keep up if you want to avoid the gators," he called back.

Lila grabbed the handle of the other bag and struggled to catch up. The wheels bumped against the uneven pavers.

"You're kidding about the alligators, right?" She cast nerv-ous glances into the shadows as they passed.

Jackson stopped so abruptly that Lila came within inches from falling over him. She felt the heat radiate from his body, and the fresh scent of saltwater filled her senses.

He'd probably been in the sun all day.

He turned to face her. In the fraction of moonlight that illumi-nated his face she could see that he was serious. "I spend most of my life out on the water. There're two things I never joke about: predatory water creatures and the one that got away."

Lila scrunched her eyebrows. He had to be kidding.

"As in . . . the *fish* that got away?" She cursed herself the moment the question came out. What if he'd been referring to some girl he'd lost his heart to? It'd be dandy for her to bring it up in the middle of a dark, unfamiliar path potentially lit-tered with deadly reptiles. She wouldn't blame him for drop-ping her luggage and letting her fend for herself.

"Could be." A slow grin spread across his features. His hon-eyed accent caressed the words. "Thing is, they never *do* get away."

A shiver darted down Lila's spine. She swallowed the lump in her throat and busied herself trying to balance her shoulder bag on top of her rolling suitcase. Jackson gave a low chuckle and continued down the path. Aggravated with herself, Lila vowed to avoid Jackson as much as possible without being rude. The last thing she needed was to be reeled in by some womanizing water ski instructor, or whatever he was.

By the time they reached the third floor of the horseshoe-shaped building that would be her new home, she appreciated Jackson's assistance with her bags. He dropped the luggage outside her room and reclined against a rail that fenced in the courtyard.

"This is you," he said. "I'm just one floor down and two rooms over."

Great. Lila ignored the excess information and dug into her pocket for the plastic key card. "If this is a guest room, how come it's so far away from the main areas?" she asked, seeking a neutral topic.

"It's not one of the better guest rooms."

"And the staff accommodations are intermingled with the guest rooms? That doesn't seem right."

"They're in the process of converting this whole building to staff rooms," Jackson explained. "Right now, we're four to a room. That's a bit snug for most of us. When they're finished, we'll be three to a room."

"Four to a room?" Cliff hadn't clued her in to that part of resort life. "How do you stand it?"

"Well, I have my own room."

"What?" Lila balked.

Jackson shrugged. "It's all about who you know. The old PR guy was a friend of mine. He used to spend summers in my hometown, so I pulled a few strings. Not everyone around here is like Jenna. I'm sure you'll like your roommates."

"*Like* them, sure. But live with three of them in a six-hundred-square-foot cracker box?"

"If you decide you can't stand it, I'm just one floor down and two rooms over," Jackson drawled, flashing a dreamy smile.

Lila gaped at him.

"If I recall," he said, more helpfully, "you're moving to Room 209 after this?"

Lila checked the printout and nodded.

"That'll be Pascalle, Regina, and Sophie. Pascalle and Sophie are both *in couple,* so you won't see much of them."

"In couple?"

Jackson placed one hand against the wall and leaned in toward Lila. Her pulse kicked up again. She inched backward and bumped against the door with a soft thud. Jackson smiled again. Lila wished he'd stop doing that.

"To be *in couple* is local Tour Paradise lingo. It means you're involved with only one other member of the staff team," he explained.

Lila swallowed the lump that'd reformed in her throat. "At a time?" she squeaked. *What had made her say that?*

Jackson's eyes twinkled with amusement, but to his credit he didn't laugh at her.

"Yes, one at a time *and* true to each other. Until they break up and go in couple with someone else, that is," he added in a matter-of-fact way.

"Is that a fact?"

Jackson shrugged. "Yeah."

"You should know *some* people believe in real commitment," Lila said. She knew she should have let it go, but she'd had enough of guys who thought long-term commitment was a dirty word. Guys like Brody.

Jackson studied Lila. So that was it. She was a woman scorned, and she had fled to Tour Paradise to escape the aftermath. She wasn't the first to try that tactic, and it worked for most of them. This corner of paradise had an abundance of willing partners to help one forget a broken heart. He surprised himself by feeling irritated by the fact as he watched Lila fumble with her room key. Something about her was too vulnerable for that approach.

A blast of cool air hit them head-on. Lila yanked the larger bag and pulled it across the threshold, but it caught on the doorjamb. Jackson reached in and lifted it across.

"It's a bit chilly in there for such a cool night. Want me to come in and adjust the thermostat?" he offered.

"You call this a cool night? I'm burning up."

Jackson grinned at the implication, and Lila turned three shades of red. Protectiveness flooded him when he saw the blush. The girl may act experienced, but she was in over her head. "Look. You're new around here, so I'll give you some well-intended advice."

Lila fixed him with tawny eyes, flecked with gold.

A fawn ready for slaughter. "Working inside the walls of this resort isn't like living in the real world. The closest thing I can compare it to is high school—but where everyone is popular, no one has any inhibitions, and there seem to be no consequences."

Lila flinched at his words. Jackson watched the flicker of uncertainty. Even in her innocence, she didn't seem senseless. Maybe he'd be able to frighten her into being on guard. He took stock of her lean figure and the sexy line of her full mouth. She stood close enough to catch the faint scent of flowers . . . lilac, maybe. She was a dangerous combination of allure and innocence. She'd need to be careful, or the sharks in this place would eat her alive, and he wasn't worried about the ones that lived in the water.

"There are guys around here who wouldn't think twice about corrupting a girl like you. When the tour buses arrive, they choose a different conquest every week—and not just the single ones. At the same time, most are rotating through the girls in the staff."

Lila crossed her arms. "This isn't high school, and I'm not some unsuspecting freshman. I'm capable of protecting my heart."

"Darling, it's not your heart they'll be after." He made a

show of speaking casually, but he didn't like the way the conversation had twisted. He wasn't making an impression.

"Thanks for your help with the luggage, but if you don't mind, I'm tired." She stifled a yawn to make the point.

Jackson decided to make one last effort, then wash his hands of it. Why was he bothering anyway? She was a stranger, and he hadn't come to Tour Paradise to babysit anyone. He had more important things to think about—or rather, to try not to think about.

"What I'm telling you is from experience. I—" Jackson started to say he'd seen it happen to a dozen girls in the staff alone.

Lila widened her eyes before he could finish. "Thanks for the warning. In that case, I will be careful, starting with *you*." She took advantage of his shock to ease him out the door and close it behind him.

Chapter Four

TO CLIMB A LADDER, YOU MUST BEGIN WITH THE FIRST STEP;
BEST TO USE A NET JUST IN CASE.
LUCKY NUMBERS: 14 2 8 16 34 9

Lila peered at the bedside clock and felt her heart leap into her throat. *How could it be after eight?* She scrambled out of bed toward the window without flicking on the light, tripping over her unpacked suitcase. *That was going to bruise.* Rubbing her shin, she tugged a pulley to open the drapes. A slice of sunlight knifed across the room. She turned and squinted through it.

A bustle of morning activity was visible through the lower leaves of a palm tree that stretched up from the ground outside her window. Clusters of golfers worked their rounds on the green in the distance. Next to the golf course, the horse stables teemed with riders returning from early-morning trail rides. On the paths weaving through the gardens under her window, people ambled by in dark glasses, kids in tow. *Definitely late. Almost a whole hour, on the first day.*

Lila ignored her throbbing shin and hobbled to the shower, emerging a record three minutes later, dripping, shivering, and wondering why she hadn't let Jackson adjust her thermostat the night prior. Then she remembered her weakness for good-looking, smooth-talking men and congratulated herself on her newly acquired good sense. Colder was better.

She jerked a comb through her hair, tying the strands into a wet ponytail. After brushing her teeth at superhuman speed

21

and swiping on a single coat of mascara, she unzipped a corner of the suitcase, now sprawled flat in the center of the room, and pulled out the first accessible outfit. Then she dug into her duffel for a pair of tennis shoes, grabbed the map, and bolted out the door.

A wall of hot, sticky air hit her head-on. She tucked a strand of droopy bangs behind her ear and backtracked along the path Jackson had taken her on the night before. It led to a cobbled walkway outside her building, where she paused to study a limp corner of the map.

If she veered right, she'd pass the main restaurant, boutique, and reception area, and eventually hit Little Delights. But if she cut through the gardens, she'd reach a side gate more quickly. Or, maybe not. She couldn't tell if the path went all the way through. If she went left, she'd intersect the walkway that snaked along the river, and that, too, would spill into Little Delights. She strained to see past the foliage and palm trunks to assess which route was shortest. She'd just decided to go left when she heard a man's voice behind her.

"Are you lost, beautiful girl?" A swarthy-looking man with an indiscernible accent stood smiling at her like a crocodile might smile at a flamingo caught snoozing at the water's edge. He wore a red shirt and crisp, white, too-short shorts.

Lila squirmed under his open appraisal. "I'm just on my way to Little Delights."

"You are forgetting something, no?"

Lila looked down in panic. Had she put something on backward in her haste?

The man looked amused. "Your little one? You do not plan to check *yourself* into Little Delights?"

He thought she was a guest. Well, fine by her. Let him think she was someone's mother, and maybe he'd leave her alone. Jackson's words cut across her thoughts. *When the tour buses arrive, they choose a different conquest every week, and not just the single ones.* Surely not someone's mother? The man seemed to look straight through her tank top, which, now damp, clung to her chest. She decided to stick with the mother shtick for as long as she could and hope for the best.

She forced a laugh. "Right. Silly of me. Can you tell me which way it is? I'd like to check it out first."

"I will escort you. My name is Guy." He pronounced his name the French way, like *gee,* and veered her to the right—the slightly longer route, by her calculation.

Don't panic. He didn't even ask my name, so probably he's not interested, anyway. It's probably his job to look out for confused tourists. Better to get there fast with an escort than wander around the grounds and make myself later.

"My dear, tell me your name," Guy said as they strolled past the restaurant.

The sweet-salty aroma of waffles and bacon filled Lila's nose. She wished she'd woken early enough for breakfast. "Lila."

A smile spread over Guy's face. "Like a flower. A name to bring a man to his knees by its beauty. *My* beauty."

His *what?* She wasn't going to be *his* beauty for all the citrus in Florida.

They turned the corner of the restaurant, and Little Delights' bright blue fence came into view. She mustered a bright tone. "I bet you say that to all the girls. Oh, look, we're here. Goodbye and thanks." She wriggled free of his grasp and made a dash for the gate, shivering with relief.

The relief didn't last; she caught sight of a sprawling playground jammed with miniature slides, swings, plastic cars, and sand toys, all backing up to a fenced-in wading pool. *What was she doing here again?* Oh yeah, her education, her future as a writer, her hopes and dreams—all within grasp but for one teensy little thing. Tuition money. Lila straightened her shoulders and approached the gate. *You can do this, Lila.*

Two staff members, a guy and a girl, stood at the middle of the playground, with preschoolers buzzing around them. Parents filed into the adjacent building, making their drop-offs.

Lila breathed the scent of sunscreen and chlorine, and she headed for the yellow building housing Little Delights. Inside, a mural of a tropical rainforest covered every inch of the walls. She scanned the room for someone in charge. A businesslike woman with strawberry blond hair and freckles sat at a table, signing in children. She looked up when she saw Lila hovering.

"Good morning! You can place your child's things in one of the cubbies, and I'll be right with you. Little Monkeys, ages two to five, are to the left; Macaws, ages six to nine, are to the right; and Panthers, age ten and older, are straight back."

"Thanks, but I'm not here to drop off a child—I'm Lila. I'm supposed to be working here for a few months?" Lila hated that her words came out like a question. She resolved to act more confident. She might not have any idea what she was doing, but she didn't need to advertise the fact to her new boss.

The woman's eyes shot to a clock on the wall, then she finished attending the parents in line. When she returned to Lila, she didn't look pleased. "You're late. I had to fill in for you this morning."

"I know. I'm sorry. I got in late last night, and I must not have set the alarm right because I—"

The woman held her hand up to stem Lila's excuses.

"Just be on time tomorrow. I'm Jules. I'm in charge of Little Delights." She looked Lila up and down. "Didn't you get the schedule?"

"I did. I don't think the alarm was even working. I—"

"I mean your clothes. You're not wearing red and white." Jules pointed at Lila's pink, ribbed tank top and her denim shorts.

"Oh," Lila said as the realization hit her. "I'm sorry. I was in such a rush. I forgot."

This wasn't going well. She wasn't used to falling short of people's expectations. She hoped word of her failed first day wouldn't get back to Cliff. She was just going to have to work extra hard to prove her worth.

"Well, it's too late to change now. We have to maintain the right staff-to-child ratio, and you're needed out there. I'll introduce you to Lacey and Ryan, and they'll let you know what to do. You're up for tennis in fifteen." Jules pulled open a drawer and handed Lila a plastic name tag with her name in beaded jewels underneath the Tour Paradise logo. "Wear your badge at all times, and I mean *all* times. It doesn't get removed until you retire for the evening. Even when you're off duty, you're on duty. If you don't know what I mean, you soon will."

"Got it. Thanks." Lila smiled to show her enthusiasm. She clipped the name tag to her tank top and patted it.

Julia strode out the door into the covered play area where a guy who would have looked more at home at a clam bake than a kiddie pool sat atop a picnic table. He observed a group of youngsters at play. A platinum blond crouched over a toddler, slathering sunscreen on the kid's dimpled cheeks. Lila noticed both staff members wore red T-shirts and white shorts. She tugged at her own pink tank top.

Jules introduced the girl first, as Lacey. She smiled as Jules handed her a roster of names. "Lacey can finish the introductions and get you started for today. I'm late to meet the costumer for the Little Delights show."

Jules hurried off, and Lacey turned the toddler around to swipe sunscreen on the back of her neck. "Little Delights puts on a weekly show for the parents. We try to make it look professional. People feel like they're getting their money's worth if they can brag that their little angel got to tap dance on stage. It doesn't even matter if they have speaking parts—as long as they look cute and dance around a little, everyone's happy. Jules takes it seriously, though."

Lila nodded. It made sense that people would love to see their kids up on stage.

"What do you think of the boss?" Lacey asked.

"She seems nice."

"She's a Harvard grad, you know." Lacey wiped residual

sunscreen on a beach towel, then shooed the toddler toward a plastic car.

"What's she doing here?"

"You'd be amazed at the people you meet working here. The tennis instructor has a law degree, the head dining room hostess has an MBA, and the wind-surf instructor speaks four languages. That's just the tip of the iceberg."

"Wow," Lila said, impressed. "But why are they *here?*"

"Why are *you* here? Look around. It's a nice little break from reality. Most will return to the real world after a season or two, but while they're here, they live in paradise."

Lila couldn't help wondering why, if the resort was so full of professionals, Jackson had made the guys sound shallow and immature.

"With so many interesting backgrounds, it must make for lots of stimulating conversation."

Lacy snorted. "It makes for lots of stimulation, that's for sure. It's a lot of ego in one place. Speaking of ego, come meet Ryan."

Ryan jumped from the picnic table. His wavy hair flopped in his eyes. He smiled, revealing too-bright teeth. "Welcome!" Ryan's voice boomed, at odds with his stature. "Always nice to meet another hottie." He mock bowed.

Lacey rolled her eyes. "She's too tall, and undoubtedly too smart, for you, Ryan, so give it a rest."

Ryan grinned and bolted to keep a kid from dumping a bucket of sand over the toddler Lacey had plastered with sunscreen.

Lacey gave Lila an impromptu orientation. "We gather in the playground every morning until everyone's signed in. They're pretty well contained here, so we just need to make sure they don't open the gate to the wading pool or something. Then we start out morning activity, usually some sport, while it's cooler. Then we come back for snack and crafts, then a nap before lunch. There's an afternoon activity, like swimming, then nap again. I love nap time."

"Sounds like fun?" Lila said. *How am I going to pull this off?*

"Well . . . *they* like it. This age group is a lot of work. The older groups are more fun. Like today, the six- to seven-year-olds are already off on a scavenger hunt. But we don't always get diaper duty. The staff rotates through the age groups to keep everyone sane and fresh. We've got this group for the week. It's not so bad—they *are* awfully cute." She bent over to ruffle the curls of a girl who was patting the ground with a plastic shovel.

Lila watched Ryan soothe a child who was on a crying jag for her mother. *Cute, right.* She peeked at the clock through the open window. Five minutes until tennis lessons. *How does one give tennis lessons to preschoolers when one doesn't know how to play tennis to begin with?*

Lacey must have interpreted the look on her face. "When they go to the formal sports programs, like tennis or tumbling, we don't have to do anything but manage crowd control. The instructors handle the rest. You'll like tennis. Henri's hot."

"Henri?"

"One of the tennis instructors."

"The one with the law degree?"

"Nah, that's Drew. Henri and Isabelle are on-again-off-again *in couple*. They broke up a few weeks ago and are still off."

"Someone thought they could do better than Isabelle?" Lila shot a look at Ryan. She felt bad, but the child wailing into his ear was grating on her nerves. How he could stand it?

"Isabelle is a lunatic. I've never met anyone less emotionally sound. Her temper is enough to frighten the Mob. She caught Henri congratulating a guest on a well-played tennis game and flipped."

Lila felt her eyebrows reach for her hairline.

"Okay, so he might've had his lips somewhere near hers in the process, but come on, he's *French*. That's what the French do, they kiss. She didn't let him explain."

"*Was* he just congratulating her on a well-played game?"

"Who knows? The resort likes us to encourage the guests a

little. If Henri came at me with those lips after a game, *I'd* let him.''

Ryan propped the bawling child on one hip and stood there smiling and bouncing her.

"Wait a minute. What do you mean the resort likes us to *encourage* the guests?" Lila had to yell to be heard.

Lacey shrugged her off, distracted by the inconsolable child. "Let me try. It's okay, sweetheart. Mommy's coming back soon. Want to go play tennis with a big, strong, handsome man?"

"Nice try," Ryan said. "But I'm staying here with the younger crowd today. No tennis for me."

"As if I could mean *you*." Lacey rolled her eyes.

Lila was reminded of a sister sparring with a younger brother.

"Hey, I'm good looking, aren't I?" he asked Lila.

Lila busied herself tying a sunhat on a girl who'd tried to pedal by on a three-wheeler. No way was she getting roped into that trap.

"You're killing my ego. Don't you think I'm just a little good looking?"

Lila sighed. "Um, sure."

"Yes!" Ryan brought his first down in a triumphant sweep. "The new girl likes me." He gave her an appraising look and blew a whistle that hung around his neck to draw the children's attention. "Little Monkeys! If you're four or five, line up behind grumpy Miss Lacey and pretty Miss Lila at the gate. If you don't know what I'm talking about, stand there and I'll round you up."

"Okay, *him* you don't have to encourage," Lacey set down the sniffling toddler and shook her head.

"About that . . . what *did* you mean when you said management likes us to encourage the guests?" Lila asked.

"Didn't you get the pep talk? You know . . ." Lacey steered the children in a straight line. "Mingling at the bar, dancing at the nightclub, drawing guests into conversation at meals . . . generally making sure they have a good time."

"*How* good a time?" Lila said with a slow feeling of dread.

"Not *that* good, unless you want to—but who'd want to when you've got all the sweets in the local candy store right under your nose? To tell you the truth, sometimes the guys dabble a bit with the tourists, but we girls usually stay away. Here, hold this." She shoved the end of a thick rope into Lila's hand and began to uncoil it. She walked through the little crowd making sure every child placed one hand on the rope.

"Okay, Little Monkeys, we're going to play a game on the way to tennis. It's called *Party Train.* If we get to the tennis courts and back without *anyone* dropping the rope, we'll have a treat for you before nap time."

Lila watched in frightened amazement while the children tightened their grips on the rope and hopped like little popcorn kernels ready to explode.

"Miss Lila will be the leader, and I'll be the caboose. You are all the train cars in between, so keep holding that rope. Go ahead, Miss Lila. Tennis courts are out the gate to the left. Chugga-chugga, choo-choo!"

Lila looked at the kids gripping the rope, then down at her own hands. How fitting; that's just how she was beginning to feel.

At the end of her rope.

Chapter Five

IT'S BEST TO FACE FACTS WITH DIGNITY;
AND AN ARSENAL OF WET WIPES.
LUCKY NUMBERS: 3 41 15 37 4 22

Tennis with fourteen jumpy Monkeys wore thin on Lila's inexperienced nerves. Distant alligators, lounging in the sun like ominous logs in the grass beyond the courts, did nothing to eliminate her nervousness. She wasn't worried they'd attack, but the sight of them reminded her of Jackson. The last thing she needed was to sit in the warm sun and let her imagination drift to his piercing eyes and Southern drawl.

Henri was a magician with the kids. The best, and critical, part, as far as Lila was concerned, was that he treated her like one of the kids. When he released the class back to Lila and Lacey, however, things spiraled out of control.

Instead of being worn out from the exercise, the children bounced in their tiny sneakers, their hands glued to the Party Train, remembering the treat that Lacey had promised. They barely made it back to Little Delights without derailing. Lila was beginning to understand why Lacey liked nap time. It was starting to sound like Happy Hour.

"Okay, Party Trainers, listen up!" Lacey called over the ruckus. "Follow Miss Lila into the clubhouse, grab a mat, and form a circle."

Lila led the pack inside. By the time they'd settled, her circle looked more like an obtuse triangle. At least they were all sitting. Lacey joined them, carrying two jugs of apple juice and a package of vanilla sandwich cookies.

"Miss Lila's going to lead you in a song while I prepare the treat," she announced, setting the jugs on a table and rummaging through a cupboard for paper cups and napkins.

"I am?" Lila didn't bother to conceal the panic in her voice.

The children squirmed. Lila forced herself to breathe through her nose in case they could sense fear, like real jungle animals.

"Just sing anything and throw in hand movements. It doesn't have to be fancy." Lacey parceled out the cookies onto napkins.

"I don't know any kid songs," Lila said.

"You must know some. 'The Littlest Worm'? 'Found a Peanut'? 'Aba Daba Honeymoon'?"

"Aba Daba what? That doesn't even *sound* appropriate."

"Criminy. Never mind. You get the snack; I'll sing. They get half a cup of apple juice and two cookies each. Let me know when you're ready."

Lila watched, impressed, as the children inched closer to Lacey, leaning forward on their knees, almost in a real circle now. They waved their arms, following Lacey's lead and trying to catch imaginary gumdrops in the air. Lila made a mental note to look up some lyrics as soon as she could get access to a computer. With a sinking feeling, she realized that might not be until she finished out the season.

Lila poured the juice. At least she could do something useful. By the time Lacey had finished singing about sunbeams, bubblegum, and ice cream, she'd whipped the kids into a froth. Lila stepped aside when the little darlings plundered the treat table.

"I'll set up the movie for nap time," Lacey said. "We took longer getting back from tennis, so we'll have to skip craft for today."

Guilt speared through Lila. If she'd exercised better control over her end of the train, they'd have gotten back on time. She opened her mouth, ready to apologize, but Lacey smiled at her.

"No biggie. I prefer nap time. Clownfish or mermaids?" Lacey held up two popular animated movies.

"I haven't seen either," Lila admitted.

"Then you *have* to see the tearjerker. Of course, you'll probably see it so often that one day you'll beg for the little clownfish to be eaten by the great white."

"He gets eaten?" A little girl blinked up at Lila. She had vanilla frosting smeared across her nose.

"Of course not, sweetheart." Lila swiped the girl's face with a wet wipe. "He doesn't get eaten, does he?"

Lacey laughed. "Alas, no. Okay, kiddos, Miss Lila is going to walk around and wipe your hands and faces; then it's time to find your nap mat in the quiet room." She looked at Lila. "I'll take diaper duty before nap, but you and Ryan will have to handle it afterwards. I'm meeting Jules at the costumer's. I'll be back before you take them to the water-ski show. It's amazing. You'll love it."

"I'm sure," Lila responded. She wondered if Jackson would be in the show.

Lila wiped away a tear when the father and son clownfish reunited. She stretched in the darkened room. At least *that* hadn't been stressful. Ryan sauntered in and winked at her. *Oh brother. Tell me this guy is kidding.* "Reporting for diaper duty?" Lila asked, deciding no one could be flirtatious over a dirty diaper.

"This is the preschool crowd. They don't need diapers," Ryan countered.

Lila sniffed the air. "Some of them do."

"Then you get the diapers, Babe. I'll take the rest to the bathroom."

"Lacey said we're supposed to work in pairs. We can let the bathroom group sleep a little longer while we work on the diapers."

Ryan frowned. "Fine, but I'm warning you—I'm not good at this."

"How hard can it be?"

Ten minutes later Lila and Ryan were soiled with the evidence of just how hard changing diapers could be. Lila's tank top had been ruined. The only clean shirt they could find was a kid's Dr. Seuss T-shirt abandoned in the lost and found. It was too snug and just covered Lila's midriff as long as she kept her arms straight down at her sides. That was impossible to do while holding a toddler. Ryan smiled when he saw her in it.

"Wow, kids, look at Miss Lila. Would you like her in a box? Would you like her with a fox?" He winked. "I know I would."

"Very original." Lila rolled her eyes.

"Hey, I told you I wasn't any good at this."

"Then what are you doing working in Little Delights?"

Ryan shrugged. "Water-ski job was already filled."

Lacey reappeared. She eyed Lila's tiny T-shirt. "Do I want to know?"

"One of the little boys had an accident while I was changing him."

Lacey shook her head. "Don't let Jules see you in that thing. We're supposed to be a little more conservative when working with the kids. On the plus side, you're likely to attract some attention from the water-ski team, and they're all so cute."

Lila wondered if a male breathed this side of the Mississippi whom Lacey didn't think was cute. "Maybe I should run back and change before we head out."

"No time. The show starts in ten minutes, and I don't want to miss Jackson's slalom solo."

Great, Lila thought. This day just keeps getting better and better.

Jackson tightened the strap of his slalom ski and eased into the water. The general manager, Tustin, had just announced the all-girl water-ski team, which performed some impressive ballet moves on trick skis. Jackson scanned the crowd on the riverbank while he waited for his cue. A good-sized mob flanked the shore, which meant a busy week for the water-ski instructors. He watched the spectators as he adjusted his ski gloves. As usual, the Little Delights sat up front. He squinted across the water at the figure sitting in the middle of the children. Lila Hayes. *Holy crap, what was she wearing?* Every hot-blooded male in Florida would be drooling over her in that Band-Aid for a T-shirt. Why wasn't she following the dress code? Hadn't Jenna told her not to be creative?

She was gutsy, all right, but she didn't know what was good for her. He turned away and tried to focus on Tustin's voice. What did he care anyway? She wasn't his problem.

The crackling voice announced Jackson just as the speedboat driver hit the gas. He lurched forward through the waves and skimmed the smooth surface of the river. A sense of euphoria overcame his earlier irritation as he concentrated on the first jump in his path. His ski hit the ramp at the calculated angle and propelled him through the air. He inverted his body into a three-hundred-and-sixty-degree flip and landed on the water with grace. The crowd roared. He spun around, placing his back to the driver, and demonstrated some backward skiing, lifting one hand from the rope to wave to the crowd.

When the driver turned the boat parallel to shore, Jackson spun forward and veered sharply to the right. Aiming for the sand, he skid to a stop just yards from the crowd, and he dropped the rope. As the boat circled back and the crowd cheered, Jackson stripped off his ski and tossed it to the side. Catching Lila's eye, he glowered at her before turning back and running into the water. He'd just latched back on to the floating rope when the driver revved toward the middle of the river. The crowd shrieked when it figured out what he was doing. Seconds later, Jackson cut through the water, barefoot.

Toward the middle of the river, he spun again and skied backward toward the pier. Just before reaching his destination, he smiled and waved, then turned to soar off the main waterway.

He streamed from the water in a hurry. He'd caught a glimpse of that worm, Guy, wedging in next to Lila on the beach. She'd looked pretty much at home sitting on the beach with a kid in her lap and five more flanking her. Good thing she had the little tykes to create a barrier between her and the four or five land sharks he'd noticed circling. He thought of her attire and shook his head. Apparently, she hadn't taken him seriously last night. He'd have to try harder to make himself clear.

Lila's eyes met Jackson's as he stormed toward her. He balked. He hadn't expected to see the flash of fear reflected in her face. He tried to soften his expression, but Guy was closing in on her. Jackson felt his nostrils flare. Bertrand from reception stopped him with a hand on his shoulder. "Jackson, hey man. I was just at reception, and you kept getting calls from some chick named Emily. She sounded sort of freaked out."

Jackson watched Lila remove a toddler from her lap and stand up to stretch. "Emmalee? When?"

"For the past hour. Wicked barefooting, by the way."

"Thanks." Pug had never disturbed him at the resort before, except for a weekly e-mail, which he expected. If she was calling, it had to be something important. He took one last, lingering look at Lila and went to call Pug.

Chapter Six

Jackson had to wait twenty minutes for the phone at reception to free up. Employees weren't allowed to use personal cell phones while on duty. Since they were pretty much always on duty, Jackson had forgotten to charge his. It'd been dead when he tried it in his room a few minutes earlier.

A blond chatting on the phone swiveled to look at him. A messy bun barely contained her spiraling hair. She wore a red tropical wrap she'd somehow managed to tie into a short dress. "Got to go. Someone needs to use the phone." When she'd hung up, she scanned Jackson from head to toe and licked her bottom lip. "Hi, Jackson. Whatcha doing?"

"Geez, Traci," was all Jackson replied. He picked up the receiver and dialed Pug's number.

"Cast-a-Line Charters and Tours," a harried voice answered.

"Pug, it's me."

"Jacky!" Pug's voice skittered up a few octaves. "I'm so glad you called. It's madness here. We've never been so busy. It must be El Niño."

"El Niño has nothing to do with our business, Pug." Jackson laughed.

"Then it's a full moon."

"You called to tell me business is good?"

36

"You already know that, Jacky. You see the numbers. That's not why I called."

Jackson couldn't help but smile and relax. If anything was wrong she'd have blurted it out by now. "Are you going to make me guess?"

"Two guesses."

"Pug, you know I don't like to play games."

"Could've fooled me—I hear they play nothing *but* games in that hyped-up high school you're hiding out in."

"I'm not hiding."

"Fine. But I notice you aren't denying the game-playing part. I thought you'd finished all that years ago."

"Pug, is there a point to this call?"

"You'll never guess."

"And I'm beginning to think you'll never tell. What's going on?"

"Well, I'm . . . getting married."

Jackson stared at the receiver, dumbfounded. *Married? Pug?*

"Hello? You didn't fall off the boat or anything, did you?"

"I'm not on my cell." Jackson struggled to compose himself. "Pug, you aren't in trouble, are you?"

"No, you schmuck. I'm in love."

"Easy, Pug. Sorry." Jackson couldn't help grinning. He missed Pug's occasional downright orneriness. It made a nice contrast to all the bogus charm he got around Encantadora. "Who'd you trap?"

"You make it sound like I got him catching crabs."

"I hope not."

"Keep it up, pretty boy. I know where to find you. It's Barney Koonz."

Jackson drew a blank.

"You know, *Fish* Koonz."

Recognition dawned. "Ah. *Fish.*"

"He started coming around after you left, asking to rent

tackle. I teased him that he was the only man named Fish who had to rent a line. He admitted he didn't need the line but had a crush on me since high school. He always assumed you and I were a couple. Then when you up and left, he figured he might stand a chance. He was happy to hear I never thought of you that way."

"When's the happy occasion?"

"That's why I called, Jackson." She hesitated. "Fish is old-fashioned, and he doesn't want to wait—well, he wants to wait, but he doesn't want to *wait*. We're eloping in Vegas next week."

"Next *week?* Are you sure you aren't in trouble?"

"Don't think I won't come down there and whoop your sorry butt if you insult me one more time."

"How quickly we forget who's in charge," Jackson teased.

"Okay, bossman, come back home and put your money where your mouth is."

"You know I can't do that yet."

"Won't do it is more like it. Come on, Jacky. Aren't you done fooling around there yet?"

"Nope. Lots more fooling around still to be done. I'm just getting started." Jackson set his jaw. Traci chose that moment to saunter by on her way back toward the boutique. She gave him a scheming wink. He grimaced, turning away from her.

"We need you here," Pug said.

"How do you mean?"

"The men your pa was working with have been hounding me to send someone out to see their properties. On a good day neither Manny nor I can be spared, but especially not now that I'm getting ready to take off for two weeks. They want some-one out by the end of the month."

"Can you even afford two weeks in Vegas?"

"As a wedding gift, Fish's momma is giving us five nights at the Silver Slots Casino. Fish has enough to pay for another two nights, then we'll camp at the KOA for the last week."

"I hear the Nevada KOA rivaled Niagara Falls for the top honeymoon destination last year," Jackson said.

"You go ahead and make fun, if you can take the whooping. But Fish and I just want to be together."

"So you need someone to cover for you at reception?"

"Nope, got it covered, if you don't mind Wanda Meeny sitting in for a while. She'll keep good records for us. Don't put stock in the story about her shoplifting the pig's head from the supermarket. She says they sold her bad shrimp and had it coming— though what she did with a whole pig's head, I don't know."

"I hadn't heard that particular story, but now that I have—"

"Worst part is, she tried to buy shrimp at the grocery in the first place when we got a van selling it fresh at every corner. I told her—"

"Pug, I'm fine with Mrs. Meeny watching the desk for two weeks. Old Kobie used her when I was off at school. She's trustworthy, if not the most congenial person."

"She does tend to get a bit ornery from time to time."

"Can't imagine what that would be like. So, what do you need me for again?"

"We can't ask Manny to flit over to Puerto Rico for a site visit, can we? He said he wouldn't mind checking out Mexico; he's got family there. Still, we need him to take out the cruiser. Not to mention he's not the most conversant type."

"I thought we had Manny on the skiff?"

"He's been nostalgic since your pa passed, and he likes to take the deep sea fishing tour. We got Big Bill on the skiff now."

"Great." Jackson ran his hand through his hair. Big Bill was the office gofer. When called for, he'd take folks to the pier for clamming or crabbing. He knew how to pilot a boat, but he rarely took one out for tours. "Any other changes I should know about?"

"You'd know about them all when they happened if you were *here,* Jacky. I'd love to have you back."

Jackson chose to ignore that. "Congratulations on the nuptials, Pug. He's a lucky and adventurous man. Send me the details for the site visits, and I'll make arrangements. Stay away from the blackjack table. I know you think you can count cards, but you're pretty much the only one who thinks so."

"That's what makes it wily."

"That's what makes you lose."

"I don't plan on leaving the room much, anyway."

"On that note, I wish you the best. Call me when you get back." Jackson stared at the phone a long moment, wondering at how much can change in so short a time when you aren't paying close enough attention. Fish was a good guy, had a good job, and kept his nose clean, so Jackson wasn't worried about Pug. He was worried about the business. If it had picked up as much as the recent earning reports said, he'd have to decide on expansion soon. He sighed as he turned away. *You can run, but you can't hide.*

Lila brushed away the sand stuck to the back of her thighs and picked up the front of the Party Train rope. She was annoyed to find her hands still shaking. *Jackson.* What business did he have looking at her like that? It was a good thing looks couldn't actually kill.

She took a deep breath and looked at Lacey to see why she hadn't given the signal to start to the restaurant for lunch yet. Lacey was bent over the far end of the rope, tending to a kid whose foot had fallen asleep. It was getting to be a long day, and it wasn't even half over. After her daytime duties, she'd have to shower and change, switch rooms, and head to the restaurant for *engaging conversation.* Just thinking about it exhausted her.

"My beauty, you've been leading me on."

Lila turned to find Guy behind her. She gave him a sour smile. "I don't think so.

"You led me to believe you were a guest here. If you'd confided you were one of us, I would have given you my extra special tour." He pronounced the c-sound in the word *special* like an *s*.

"Must've been a sixth sense," Lila responded. She didn't want to be rude, but she wanted less to leave anything open for interpretation.

"You wound me, Lila." Guy crossed his hands over his chest in mock pain. "Why don't you like me?"

A maddening sense of fairness tugged at Lila. Sure, Guy was a bit slimy, but maybe it was her recent prejudice against men fueling her hostility, not him specifically. She sighed. "I don't mean anything by it. This morning, I was running late, and right now I've got work to do." She gestured toward a four-year-old boy who was pulling on her hand, looking pale.

Guy grinned, showing shining white teeth against his dark skin. "I am happy to hear you are not opposed to getting to know me better. Shall we meet at the bar tonight? I'll be the one in the black shirt." He laughed at his own joke.

Lila knew everyone had to wear some combination of black or white every night. She opened her mouth to tell him no, as the boy who'd been yanking on her hand vomited on Guy's pristine white tennis shoes.

"Watch it, boy!" Guy scowled, attempting to shake the mess from his feet.

Lila gave Guy a death stare and crouched down to comfort the child. His Little Monkey's name sticker read *Jonathan*. She gently rubbed his back until he finished getting sick. Then she used her foot to cover it up with sand and tried to silence the other children from jumping around exclaiming how yucky it was. Two more children went pallid. Lila didn't want to chance any chain reactions. She called to Lacey to get moving fast.

Jonathan had tucked his tiny hand into Lila's at the front of the train. The last she'd seen, Guy remained at the river, trying to wash his soiled shoes. Even though she felt sorry for

Jonathan, she couldn't help but smile a little as they chugged away.

Jackson had looped back along the river path on his way to the boat. As he rounded the restaurant, he got a view of Lila and Guy in discussion. He would have felt better if Lila wouldn't speak to Guy at all. The guy didn't need encouragement. If the cute little kid in the Dolphins' jersey hadn't thrown up on Guy's shoes, Jackson might have had to intervene. *My sentiments exactly, kid.* He watched Lila lead the Little Delights toward the restaurant. Something stirred in the pit of his stomach as he took in the Dr. Seuss shirt stretched taut across her abdomen. He shook it off and made a mental note to see how she was turned out in the evening before deciding whether or not to give her more warnings. *No need to get involved if I don't have to.*

Chapter Seven

YOU HAVE A QUIET AND UNOBTRUSIVE NATURE;
WHAT ARE YOU DOING HERE?
LUCKY NUMBERS: 25 11 19 2 33 8

Lila wiped ketchup on her shorts from the mini-hamburgers she'd just served. She already had sand, frosting, glitter, and something she chose to assume was paste in her hair, on her shorts, and on the hem of the borrowed shirt. A little ketchup just rounded off the look.

"Is it always like this?" She scanned Ryan. His clothes were spotless, and she couldn't blame it on him not doing any work. He'd already served two tables to her one.

Ryan shrugged. "You learn how to keep a safe distance from things that drip, squirt, and ooze."

A tiny hand tugged on the hem of Lila's shorts, adding a nice stain of chocolate sauce to her collection. When she looked down, she saw it was Jonathan.

"I don't feel good, Miss Lila," he said. His eyes pleaded for her to make it better.

"Jonathan, you didn't have ice cream, did you? What happened to the soup I gave you?"

Jonathan managed to look innocent in spite of the fudgy evidence on his cheeks. "My tummy hurts."

Running the risk of another *incident* in the lunchroom was a bad idea. The kids' section was separated from the main restaurant by nothing more than a rope partition. The other side

43

was already filling up with people ready to enjoy a midday meal.

Ryan answered before Lila could ask. "Go ahead and take care of it. Lacey and I can cover out here."

Lila led Jonathan by the hand to the restrooms.

"I'm tired, Miss Lila," he told her after twenty minutes.

"I know, honey. Are you feeling any better?"

Jonathan shook his head.

"Okay, well, you just take it easy. You're going to be fine. Mr. Ryan said he'd call your parents to pick you up."

"My daddy's golfing today."

"Your mommy, then."

"Mommy's home with her new hus—husband."

"Well, I'm sure they'll find your daddy. Just try to relax, sweetie."

"Miss Lila?"

"Yes, Jonathan?"

"I love you."

Lila blinked at the mussed-up hair on the back of the little head she had been holding steady over the toilet for what'd felt like eternity. *He loved her?* Warmth swarmed her heart. Somebody loved her. Sure, he was nineteen years her junior and had known her for less than eight hours, but she had no doubt he meant it.

"Thank you, Jonathan. You're pretty special to me too."

"You don't think I'm yucky?"

"Nope. Everyone gets sick sometimes. I think you're the coolest."

"I feel better now."

Lila used a paper towel to clean Jonathan up the best she could, but tracking down Jonathan's dad was trickier. He had joined another party on the golf course and had turned off his cell phone. It took a while to reach him. Lila wanted to meet the father of her new little buddy, but she'd been busy attempting some semblance of cleaning up herself when he came to pick up Jonathan.

"This is hopeless," she said to Lacey, walking out of the restroom and dabbing her top with a wet wipe.

"You're a mess all right, but the first day is always the roughest."

"You're just saying that so I come back tomorrow."

"True. But it can only get better, right? On the bright side, only five minutes until the club closes for the afternoon. Then you'll have a whole two and a half hours to rest for tonight."

"Um . . . I think I'm excused from the evening duties this week."

"Lucky. I've got Twilight duty tonight."

"Sounds relaxing?" Lila had no doubt Twilight duty was something she'd end up with sooner or later too.

Lacey harrumphed. "It means you get to come back to take the kiddies to dinner and practice for the show. Then you gather them up for quiet time." She made mock quotation marks around the last two words. "Meaning we watch a movie while the parents hit the nightclub. All this pleasure doesn't end until you get off duty around eleven. Nine-thirty if you're one of the lucky few who get to cut out early."

"When do you eat?"

"If you work until eleven, it's mini-burgers with the kiddies. If you get off at nine-thirty, the Little Delights group hooks up in the main dining room after it closes. The chef always keeps something warm until ten, and there's plenty of wine left to dull the memories."

"That's a lot of hours."

"That's why we're so glad to see you. Usually, they avoid making us pull an all-day shift and work Twilight too. The Twilight staff typically has the mornings free—if you can call it that. Speaking of free, it's four o'clock. I'll talk to you later."

Lacey shot through the door. Ryan gave Lila a high five

before following. Jules looked up from the table where she was signing kids out to their parents. "I've got this, Lila. You can go. I hear you did a good job today." She smiled, looking like an all-American ad for apple pie. "We'll see you tomorrow—in the proper attire, I hope."

Lila blushed at both the compliment and the reminder. She could barely stifle the desire to crawl into a shower and then into bed, but she had roommates to meet. Plus, although she was off duty, she was required to dine with the guests. She wanted to spend time updating her journal, but it'd have to wait.

Lila stood outside Room 209. She raised her hand to knock on the door, even though she'd retrieved a key from Bertrand at the front desk. Her hand froze midair at the muffled conversation behind the door. It included a male voice. The talking stopped, and Lila found it too silent for comfort.

Great. She held her breath and knocked on the door, three raps in succession.

"Go away," a man exclaimed. A soft voice chastised him.

"Be right there . . . ," a woman called.

Lila willed the burning in her face to recede, but she could feel it to the tips of her ears. She'd had roommates before. This wasn't the first embarrassing encounter she'd almost walked in on, but usually they'd at least been introduced.

A stunning woman with dark hair in a braid down her back answered the door in stretchy shorts and a form-fitting tank top. *Another Isabelle, but taller.*

She gave Lila a sunny smile. "You must be Lila. I'm Pascalle, yoga instructor. We didn't think you'd be along until closer to dinner." She looked Lila over before throwing the door open and stepping aside. "It looks like you're *wearing* dinner."

Lila stepped over the threshold and diverted her eyes from the man perched on the edge of a cot—which wasn't easy in the small room. She was glad to find him dressed in a tennis uniform. "I'm Lila, Little Delights," she said.

"You'd be more delightful if you had better timing," the man said.

"Don't be rude, Drew," Pascalle said. "Lila, Drew is one of the tennis pros."

"Charmed. Got to go." He grabbed his racket from the floor.

"Sorry to have interrupted," Lila said, chagrined.

"Nonsense. You live here too. Do you need help with your bags?" Pascalle asked.

They stacked Lila's suitcases into a corner by her twin roll-away cot.

"Where is everyone else?" Lila asked.

"Sophie is a hostess, so she gets to the restaurant early. Even if she didn't have to, she would. She's *in couple* with the pastry chef. They're in love," she said, with the hint of a smile. "You won't see much of her. And Regina, well . . . Regina is Regina. She's not exactly—"

Before Pascalle could finish the sentence, another girl clipped through the door. She gave Lila an uninterested glance before heading to the shower.

"Darn, I was looking forward to that," Lila muttered.

"Meeting Regina?" Pascalle asked, surprised.

"Taking a shower."

"How many?" a sweet-looking girl with hair cut in a fashionable bob asked Lila. She wore a black dress that hugged her throat in a mock turtleneck but was cut out at the shoulders. A dusting of powder made her skin glimmer. Lila felt frumpy in her black, spaghetti-strap summer dress that skimmed her knees, even if it was supposed to be a classic.

"Just one." Lila cast her eyes around the room. She might've preferred working a double Twilight shift to conversation with a table of strangers. Her chest felt tight.

The girl contemplated Lila's name tag. "You're *Lila!* I'm Sophie. Welcome, roomie."

"It's nice to meet you." Lila forced a nervous smile.

"I'll take care of you tonight. I'll seat you with a fun table."

"Actually, I'd rather—"

"Come with me." Sophie sashayed across the room toward a half-filled table. She passed a group well into their dinner. Jackson sat there, next to a blond who looked to be hanging on his every word. In fact, the whole table laughed, entertained by whatever he was telling them. Lila caught something about a swordfish and sunburn. He paused to watch her pass, then continued without missing a beat.

Sophie deposited Lila at a table of three guys, beer-chugging types, and a dark-haired man wearing a trendy black shirt. Sophie positioned Lila in the empty seat next to the dark-haired man.

"Enjoy your dinner." She winked.

One of the beer drinkers ogled Sophie and whistled as she walked away. The man with the dark hair gave her a quiet smile. Lila decided he was the lesser of conversation risks.

"Hi, I'm Lila," she ventured.

"Joshua Knight." He held out his hand.

The frat boys put their heads together and made comments under their breath as they gawked at Lila. She shifted in her chair so she was facing Joshua.

"So, you work here, Lila?" he asked.

"I work in the Little Delights club. You?"

He looked surprised. "No."

"I'm sorry. I thought maybe the black shirt—"

"I'm a restaurateur. We tend to wrap ourselves in black." He smiled.

One of the beer drinkers sniggered.

"Wait, *Miss Lila* from Little Delights?" Joshua asked. "My son, Jonathan, raved about you. He may have a serious case of puppy love. I can see why."

Lila felt her cheeks redden, but not uncomfortably. Joshua didn't feel threatening.

"You're Jonathan's dad. I had hoped to meet you this afternoon. What a coincidence we should be seated together. How's Jonathan feeling?"

"Not great—which is why I'm dining alone. I'd planned to have him spend half his time in the club and the rest with me, but he conked out early tonight. He's with a babysitter in the room."

"I'm sorry. I hope he'll be as good as new tomorrow. He's a sweet boy."

"He'll be bummed if he misses out on swimming with Miss Lila."

"Is that what's on the agenda tomorrow?"

"Right after Monkey tumbling."

Lila smiled at him. Talking to Joshua was beginning to take her mind off the mandatory mingling. It wasn't so bad. She just hoped she wouldn't get into any trouble if she didn't engage *all* the guests at the table. Sophie brought a couple who looked to be in their late twenties to fill in the empty seats on the other side of Joshua. He made polite introductions, then turned back toward Lila.

"Shall we get something to eat?" Joshua indicated the buffet line.

"Sure."

The buffet selection was much better than the one in the kids section. Lila selected grilled mahi-mahi in coconut sauce, marinated artichoke hearts, and a side of wild rice. When they returned to the table, Lila watched Joshua over the top of her glass and realized this part of her job description wasn't as bad as she'd anticipated. She even managed to make conversation with the couple next to Joshua. She told them about her writing aspirations. When they were the only two left at the table, lingering over coffee, Joshua expressed an interest in seeing her writing sometime. When he suggested the nightclub, she agreed. It was part of her job to make an appearance there, anyway. She looped her arm through Joshua's, hardly noticing Jackson watching her from two tables away.

* * *

"I thought you hated men." Jackson's voice shot over Lila's shoulder. Joshua had gone to fetch a second round of drinks. Lila whirled to face Jackson and almost lost her balance on the slick floor. Jackson caught her by the upper arm. She could feel the strength of his grip soak through her bare skin and wondered why it was such a pleasant sensation. Before she could ponder it too long, he released her.

Jackson was close. *Too close*. She'd seen him dancing with the tall blond for the past half hour and was surprised that he still smelled like the ocean.

"I—I never said I hated men." Lila tried to remember what conversation she'd had with Jackson about men. With Jackson this close, she was having difficulty remembering her room number.

"Ha!" Jackson said, too loudly for the space between them. "You said you weren't some naive little thing that was going to get her heart broken. You said you were going to stay away from players."

"Um, I think I said I was going to stay away from *you*."

Joshua chose that moment to return with her cola. He placed the glass in front of Lila and smiled at Jackson.

"Fine. Play it that way." Jackson stormed back to the blond. *What just happened?*

"Friend of yours?" Joshua asked.

"No."

"Too bad. He's cute."

Lila looked at Joshua and groaned.

"What? You didn't think . . . ," he started to say.

Lila dropped her head in her hands. "Jonathan threw me off."

"I've learned a lot about myself since Jonathan's mother."

"That's probably why I like you so much. I must have sensed you're risk-free . . . to me anyway."

Joshua gave her a broad smile. "Dance?"

"I'm a terrible dancer."

"Humor me." He pulled her across the room and carved out a space where he demonstrated that at least *he* could dance well.

The salsa rhythm beat through Lila. She did her best to shake her hips and bob her head at the right intervals, but she knew she was a pathetic sight. After a few minutes, it didn't matter. She decided it felt too good to care if she made a fool of herself.

"I hope I'm not cramping your style," she said after they'd danced to two songs in a row.

"I'm on vacation with my four-year-old son. I'm here to *relax,*" Joshua assured her. "Okay, Trixie, spin."

He held his hand over her head and coaxed her into a spin. For a long, frozen moment, when her back was to Joshua, she caught Jackson's eye from across the floor. He was still dancing with the tall blond. Without releasing Lila's gaze, he slid his hand down the back of the blond's low-cut dress and planted a kiss on her neck. The blond reeled in surprise and pulled him to her lips. Lila snapped her eyes away. She shook from head to toe, heart pounding by the time she faced Joshua again.

"You all right?" Joshua asked.

She nodded but tears pricked her eyes.

"Better sit this one out." Joshua led her back to their table and asked if she might prefer to call it a night.

Nodding wordlessly, she followed him out of the nightclub, holding his hand for support.

She'd been swallowed up by the darkness of the winding pathways by the time Jackson made his way outside after her.

Chapter Eight

Lyrics about lying eyes and thin disguises erupted from the alarm clock, goading Lila. Her eyes flew open and she found herself staring at a bare foot sticking out from the covers across from her. A toe ring gleamed on one of the painted toes. Lila lay still while her mind pieced together where she was. She couldn't understand why her head pounded. She hadn't had anything alcoholic to drink, so why did it feel like she was being pricked by a million needles?

A hand slapped the alarm's snooze button. Regina threw back the covers. Her eyes flickered in Lila's direction, then narrowed as she padded toward the bathroom. Lila mourned access to the bathroom. *This is beginning to feel like a bad pattern.* She read the clock. 6:02 A.M. At least she had plenty of time to get ready, if she could manage to move without pain. She looked at Pascalle's empty bed. *Yoga must be for the bright-eyed.* Fortunately, watching people's kids didn't start until after breakfast.

Watching people's kids. Joshua. What had happened last night? A sense of something gone wrong crept over Lila. Something with Joshua? No, Joshua had been a perfect gentleman. She smiled as she thought of her new friend. The effort hurt her

52

face. *Should being dehydrated hurt this much?* No, it wasn't Joshua. *Jackson.* Jackson had upset her.

Lila heard the shower turn off and a blow dryer kick in.

Had Jackson accused her of playing a game? Of being a player? No . . . he . . . *the blond!* It all came back. Jackson had accused her of hanging out with a player, then he'd groped the blond right in front of her. While *looking* at her! Lila shriveled at the memory, then straightened. What difference did it make to her if he kissed some random blond? She didn't care.

Regina strode back into the room wearing a navy blue tank top and white thong underwear, acting as if Lila wasn't even in the room.

"Hi." Lila's voice was hoarse from the early hour. "I'm Lila."

Regina looked straight through her, then began sorting through a pile of clothes on the floor near her bed. She pulled out white cut-off denim shorts and slipped her legs into them.

"Your new roommate—" Lila tried again.

Regina didn't answer. She picked up a mesh tote bag, slung it over her back, and walked out the door.

"Oookay then," Lila said when the door had closed. "You have a great day too."

She swung her legs over the side of the bed, and it became obvious why her skin hurt. Her legs were sunburned a tender pink. In her rush yesterday she hadn't put on sunscreen. A girl from Arizona should know better. She sighed, making her way to the bathroom. She wiped a circle into the fog covering the mirror and recoiled from the sight of her face. It was bright pink, too, with a white streak on her chin where she'd spent most of the afternoon wearing glitter glue.

Lila opened the closet cupboard and downed a bottle of lukewarm water, then stepped under a warm shower. Ten steamy minutes later, she felt almost human again. She couldn't do much about her face; she didn't wear foundation or powder, so she couldn't try to cover it up. She'd have to go out as is. She did put an extra layer of sunscreen over every inch of her face, arms, and legs, and she spent an extra five minutes on eye make-up to draw attention away from her skin.

The schedule said it was blue and white day. Remembering she'd be taking the kids swimming, she slipped a navy blue halter top and a pair of white shorts over her bikini. She strode back to the bathroom to check the final effect and balked when she saw the farmer's tan—or rather, burn—on her arms. She thought about covering up with a T-shirt, but then she'd be stuck with it all season. She might as well try to even it out. She wiped some of the sunscreen off her shoulders and replaced it with a lower coverage.

The wall of heat greeting her outside wasn't as bad as it'd been the day before. Maybe she was already acclimating. She made her way downstairs and across the courtyard. A bird cawed somewhere in the distance, and the sound of clinking silverware wafted from the restaurant along with the smell of bacon. Her stomach growled, then lurched. She needed food before last night caught up with her.

As she meandered along the path, she made a mental note to start writing descriptions of this place in her journal. She'd have to start getting up early every day so she could sit by the river and write. She yawned. Or maybe she'd find time before dinner each night.

"Morning, Lila!" Sophie looked fresh in a bright blue sundress with white strappy sandals. She led Lila to a table in the center of the dining room. Unfortunately, the group included Jenna. Lila chose the chair furthest from her, next to a guy wearing cut-off jean shorts and high tops. Lila wasn't too surprised when he introduced himself as Bruno. She introduced herself around the table.

"Lila's a pretty name. Like a flower," Bruno said, in a thick Jersey accent. He sounded sensitive for a guy wearing a half-inch gold chain around his neck. "Has anyone told you, you got the prettiest eyes? Not many girls can wear their eye makeup like that. It sets off the gold flecks."

Lila wondered how he could notice her eyes when he kept staring in the vicinity of her chest. At least he wasn't looking at her sunburn.

Jenna vocalized part of that thought. "I'm surprised anyone would notice your eyes when you've got the goober-tan thing going."

Lila ignored her and poured a glass of water from the pitcher in the center of the table. *Sun and hard work sure did make a person thirsty.* After she gulped it down, she stood to get breakfast. Everyone declined her offer to get them something except Jenna, who'd taken to ignoring her right back. Lila made her way to the buffet line. Bruno followed.

"I wouldn't have cinnamon rolls if I was you," he said.

"Why not?" Lila asked, before thinking better of it.

"Because next to you, they ain't sweet enough."

Lila didn't bother to hide her eye rolling.

"I admit that was lame, but I'm just a guy going out on a limb here. I think you're pretty special and was wondering if you might think I could be special too."

What was with men around here and being special? Maybe they all needed a special place to be locked up.

"Bruno, you've known me for all of three minutes. How could you know I'm special?" Lila passed by the rolls and made her way to the omelet station. The man behind the counter smiled at her when she approached. His name tag read EMILIO—PASTRY CHEF. So *this* was Sophie's pastry chef. Lila knew they made use of everyone on the staff wherever they needed. Emilio had a skill for cracking more than Sophie's heart.

"Good morning." Lila smiled. "I'd like a two-egg cheese omelet with mushrooms, please."

Emilio nodded and started the flame under one of the empty omelet pans.

Bruno cleared his throat. "I could tell you was special by the way you smiled when you sat down. It said, 'I'm not just hot, I'm friendly too. Come get to know me better.' "

"No. *That* particular smile said, 'I'm starving, and I have a long day ahead of me, so I'm just here to eat my breakfast and tolerate the minimal small talk, thank you very much.' "

Bruno wasn't deterred. "I saw you dancing in the nightclub. You've got to dump Mr. I'm-Too-Sexy-For-My-Shirt and dance with a real man tonight."

Lila wondered if he was talking about Joshua or Jackson. They were the only men she'd been near in the disco. Jackson, probably; he fit the description better. As she pondered this, a tall figure clad in a faded blue, PADI dive shirt that stretched across his chest stepped into the space between Lila and Bruno.

"*Sweet pea,* why didn't you wake me before you left? I had plans for this morning." Jackson held Lila by the shoulders. He bent his head, and before Lila realized what was happening, he placed a slow, warm kiss on her parted lips.

The world around Lila ceased to exist. Bruno disappeared. The pain of her sunburn disappeared. Emilio flipping the omelet disappeared. Even the little impression of hurt that Jenna's earlier cutting remarks had made disappeared. All Lila knew was the slight zap of awareness and the salty-sweet taste of Jackson's lips caressing hers.

He pressed his mouth lightly at first, then more firmly. Lila's head buzzed, and she had to fight the urge to wrap her arms around his neck and open up to him. With every ounce of self-control, she pushed away. Jackson looked dazed, his eyes hazy and cheeks flushed. The look of sleepy satisfaction he'd had before he kissed her had been replaced by genuine surprise. *Why would he look surprised when I'd been the one ambushed?* Lila turned away and found Emilio grinning at them. Embarrassed, she turned back to Jackson. She opened her mouth but no words would form.

Jackson composed himself. "You're welcome."

"You . . . I . . . *what?*" Lila sputtered.

"I got rid of him, didn't I?" Jackson indicated the empty spot where Bruno had been. Lila looked at her table. Bruno gathered up his things and made haste toward the exit. He picked up his pace to keep up with a redhead on his way out.

"I didn't need you to get rid of him," Lila said.

"You don't mean you liked him?" Jackson's eyes were wide with disbelief.

"I'll never know now, will I?" Lila thanked Emilio for her plate and strode toward her table.

Jackson followed. "C'mon, Lila, I was doing you a favor. I've seen Jersey guy over there hit on everything in a skirt. Trust me, he's used to rejection."

"That's not the point. The point is I don't need you to—"

"Hi, *Jacky.*" Jenna stopped in front of Jackson.

Apparently she hadn't seen the kiss, Lila thought. Or maybe she had.

Jackson didn't break eye contact with Lila.

"There's an empty spot at my table if you're interested." Jenna told him.

"Yeah, sure, Jenna. Thanks," he said.

Lila knew full well he'd seen her at the table too. Jenna's eyes lit up, and she gave him a possessive look from under her lashes. Lila turned away without another word. Once seated back at the table, she proceeded to shovel down her omelet.

"Here." Jackson took the seat nearest Lila. He reached into his pocket and handed her a thin, rolled-up paper bag.

"Jackson, over here." Jenna indicated the chair next to her.

"Thanks, I'm good. Open it," he said to Lila.

Lila hesitated.

"Open it." He forked a bite of eggs into his mouth and chewed as he watched her.

Lila folded back the top of the bag as if something might jump out and bite her. *What could he have to give me?* She peeked inside at a tube of pure aloe vera gel.

"I saw you starting to turn pink last night. If you put the aloe on soon, you won't peel. It'll help with any pain too."

Lila stared at the tube and tried to reconcile this kind act with the man she'd been so annoyed with a moment earlier.

"Take it. No strings attached. It's my way of saying I'm sorry for last night."

Jenna straightened in her chair. Lila guessed she didn't like the possibility something had happened between them last night.

Lila toyed with pulling a stunt like Jackson had just done with Bruno to put Jenna off, but rejected it when she thought about having to kiss Jackson again. That would be far too dangerous.

Lila burned to ask Jackson about last night, but she didn't want to discuss it in front of Jenna. "I'd better get going." She murmured her thanks, pocketed the tube, and smiled around the table.

Before she could step away, Jackson circled his fingers around her wrist. "We'll finish our conversation later."

He released her, and she rubbed the spot on her wrist where Jackson had touched her. It burned worse than her sunburn. Lila hurried toward the exit. She almost looked forward to a day of chaos to help clear her head.

Chapter Nine

R oar!" Jonathan yelled from behind the lion mask. "Did I scare you, Miss Lila?"

"You bet. You sounded like a real lion," Lila told him. Satisfied with the response, Jonathan ran off to spin in circles, trying to catch his tail.

Lila laughed and surveyed the scene. Every child age two to six pranced around in an animal costume. "They really only have the next three days to practice?" she asked Lacey.

"After that, it's showtime, ready or not!" Lacey did a little tap dance move in place.

Lila gave her a grim look.

"Just remember, if they manage not to fall off the stage, we're doing good."

"New girl," a voice boomed from the back of the theater. Lila, Lacey, and Ryan looked up. An Asian-American man stalked toward the stage. "I need you in the show this week."

"Um, I'm supposed to be exempt," Lila said.

"I'm Patrick, the choreographer. As of today, I say you're *un*-exempt. Regina has strep throat. Someone needs to play the Dark Witch in *That Wizard of Ours* production Saturday."

"But I—"

"You're available. You'll do. Come get fitted for her costume." He gestured for Lila to follow him backstage.

Lila looked to Lacey and Ryan for help, but they only shrugged. Apparently, Patrick had seniority. She followed him backstage. He plucked a costume from a long rack and handed it to her. Lila fingered the sheer black fabric. She thought it might work better in a burlesque show than in a family theatrical production. "I can't act." She calculated just how much of her skin would show. *Way too much, from the looks of it.*

"You don't have any lines. You just have to dance with the wizard of the forest at the end."

"I'm *really* not good at dancing."

"We'll improvise. You can meet me an hour before dinner every night the rest of this week to practice."

By the time Lila rejoined Lacey and Ryan, they had the kids in a circle singing a jungle version of "Old MacDonald."

"Well?" Lacey asked.

"He wants me to take Regina's part in the show," Lila said.

Lacey raised an eyebrow. "It could be worse. I have to be a forest shadow following the wizard around wherever he goes. The role is invisible. At least you get to try to seduce him with your dance."

"Seduce him? I think I'd rather be invisible. You wouldn't want to trade?"

"Sorry. I'm not a fan of Guy."

"*Guy* is the forest wizard? And I thought this day started out bad."

"It gets worse." Lacey tried to look sympathetic but didn't quite pull it off between roars.

"How do you mean?"

"Jenna is the Enlightened Witch who throws off the Dark Witch in the finale. I've seen the way Jenna looks at you. I'd watch my back."

Lila sighed. "Just my luck."

"It's not all bad."

"How do you figure?"

"Jackson works your ropes behind the scenes." Lacey paused to fake-fan herself, then made arm movements like an elephant.

Is there no end to the horror? Lila didn't care what the ropes were for. The fact that Jackson controlled them was dismal news enough.

Jackson's shorts vibrated for the third time in an hour. He knew he was breaking the rules by having his phone with him, but he also knew he'd have time to kill while he waited for Little Delights to join the afternoon boat tour. He looked at the text message from Pug. Mr. Ramirez wanted an answer by next Sunday. Only five days away. He wouldn't be able to put off the trip to Puerto Rico any longer. Mr. Ramirez was play- ing the fear-of-loss card, saying he had two other buyers and needed to make a sell decision by the end of the month. Jack- son was tempted to let it go, but it was his father's dream, and he couldn't quite bring himself to brush it off. It was a good thing that Tustin, the general manager, was a good guy. They'd hit it off from the beginning. If Jackson talked to him soon, he was sure he could arrange a few days off next week.

A familiar sense of guilt tugged at Jackson. *Maybe it's time to stop this charade and go back for good.* He looked up from his perch in the driver's seat and across the sparkling expanse of the river. A snowy egret scanned the surface and dipped under to spear a frog. The sun warmed Jackson's face, and a sense of calm enveloped him. *No. It doesn't feel like time to leave just yet.*

A dozen chirping voices snapped him from his reverie. The familiar Party Train was headed toward the dock. His spirits dipped when he saw Ryan, not Lila, leading them. They picked up again when Lila came into sight, taking up the caboose. Two youngsters hung on each of her elbows. Warmth flowed through him as his mind flashed to their kiss in the dining room.

When he had seen her with Bruno, Jackson had only in- tended to scare Bruno off with a few well-chosen words, but when she parted those pouty lips in surprise, he couldn't resist carrying it a step further. She looked taken aback when he kissed her, but he was the one caught off guard. The electric rush he'd felt the instant their lips met staggered him. He didn't like feeling out of control.

Jackson tore his mind from the memory and focused on the approaching group. A few of the parents towed along for the ride. He forced his smile in place when he saw that Joshua was one of them.

As the children huddled on the dock, Jackson stepped off the platform of the thirty-four-foot Navigator tour boat and slid the lid off a crate of life jackets. "Hey there, Little Delights!" he called. "I'm Jackson, and I'm going to be your captain today." He smiled and ruffled the hair of a four-year-old near the front of the group. The children took an instant liking to Jackson. "I'm going to need some helpers today, so I want you to wear one of these special *first mate* life jackets. Moms and dads, you can help too." He started handing life jackets around. "Little Delights leaders, I need you up front." He motioned for Ryan and Lila to join him.

"Dude. You were wicked in the ski show yesterday. Could you show me the barefoot move?" Ryan asked.

Jackson slapped him on the back. "I'm not a water-ski instructor, Ryan. I need you to stand in the boat at the top of the ladder and get the kids seated as I hand them up."

"Right. All right, man. We'll talk later."

"Lila," Jackson turned to Lila, who had already buckled a half-dozen kids into their jackets. He started working on the group nearest him. "You want to help me hand the kids up to Ryan?"

Lila nodded, looking taken aback by something.

A little girl in a ponytail looked up at him with a quivering lip. "What if I fall in? Will the alligators and sharks get me?"

Jackson chucked her chin. "Sunshine, you're not going to fall in on my watch. Besides, you're wearing a super-special vest with alligator and shark repellent. That means it keeps them away from you. You're going to be safe with me."

The girl gave him a toothless smile. "Can I sit by you?"

"It just so happens I have a co-pilot chair right next to mine. I was hoping a brave little girl like you would volunteer to sit there. Stand over to the side with Miss Lila. I'll bring you up last with me."

Lila caught his eye for a moment, her forehead creased in either concentration or confusion, before turning away to hand another child up to Ryan. When almost everyone was seated, Jackson held out his hand to help Lila up the ladder.

She hesitated before placing her hand in his. She was soft and warm. He caught a light floral scent coming off her hair and resisted the urge to lean in and bury his nose in the strands. She caught his eye again, and Jackson saw a flicker of fear, but she turned away and headed toward the back of the boat to tend to the children before he could ask about it.

As Jackson untied the boat from its mooring, Traci skipped up in a lacy swimsuit cover-up, trimmed on top with ridiculous feathers. It barely contained her. "Got room for one more, Jackson?"

Jackson sighed. Using her to get to Lila last night had been a mistake, not that he was thinking clearly at the time. "Sorry, Traci, I think we're full."

Ryan's voice boomed from above. "I've got one seat open by me. Send her up."

Traci grabbed Jackson by the arm and held on longer than necessary to get up the steps. "Can't I sit up here by you?"

"I already have a co-pilot." Jackson indicated the little girl who was waiting, puffed up proud, to board.

Traci leaned into him. "You don't know what you're missing." She shimmied up the ladder.

Want to bet? Jackson held out a hand for the little girl in the life jacket. "Ready, partner?"

Lila had to admit she was impressed by the way Jackson managed the Little Delights boat tour. She hadn't even known he could drive a boat of that size. She'd assumed he was just another water-ski jock. She hadn't expected him to be a natural with the kids. They loved him and the stories he told about the river's wildlife. He made the trip through the winding river a real adventure. Lila was disappointed when the tour ended. The only drawback had been the tall blond she'd seen Jackson with the night before, Traci. She'd flaunted herself at him the whole time. To Jackson's credit, he had maintained his professional demeanor and kept redirecting attention outside the boat. Still, it was a bit much. More than one fascinated daddy disembarked with more than one annoyed mommy when it was over.

Jackson gave all the kids high fives on their way down, and everyone saluted his co-pilot. He even let the little girl keep a pair of his sunglasses that she couldn't bear to part with.

"You don't have to do that," Lila said, as she brought up the rear of the troop.

"What, the glasses? I've got a dozen pairs. She makes them look better than I do, anyway." He gave her a genuine smile. It was clear he enjoyed being with the kids.

"That's debatable," Lila mumbled under her breath.

"What was that?"

"Nothing," Lila lied. "Thanks for the tour. It was good. *You're* really good . . . with the kids."

Jackson squinted at her through the sun, as if trying to pick something out of her head. "But how am I doing with you?"

"You mean Traci."

"I mean you."

"Jackson!" Traci called from the dock below. "Can you help me with this life jacket? I think the buckle's stuck." She gestured helplessly toward the clasp near her chest.

"Duty calls. Thanks again." Lila stepped off the boat before Jackson could respond. She distracted herself with rounding up the remaining exhausted Little Delights.

Lila heard Jackson address Traci with exasperation. "Traci, we need to talk."

Chapter Ten

USE YOUR HEAD, BUT LISTEN TO YOUR HEART;
UNLESS YOU CAN'T TAKE THE BEATING.
LUCKY NUMBERS: 4 27 40 33 25 2

The colors of the sunset played against Lila's eyelids while classical music floated around her. It almost felt like vacation. Lila let the air out through her nose and opened her eyes. She'd found this corner of paradise by accident. She'd been returning from a disastrous first rehearsal with Patrick, anxious to get back to her room and bury her head under a pillow. When she'd cut across the back of the restaurant, she'd discovered that the resort played classical music on the deck overlooking the river at sunset. She'd been shocked to find the place empty. Everyone must either take the shuttle to the ocean for sunset or spend this time primping for the evening's events. *Okay by me. I can finally carve out some time to write in my journal in peace.*

She had so much to write about. She thought of the feelings surrounding her breakup with Brody, the fears and uncertainties of coming to Encantadora, and the roller-coaster ride she'd been on since. She had a few snappy sayings floating around her head that needed to be written down before she forgot them. Those offbeat quotations tended to pop into her mind during times of stress. It relaxed her and helped keep things in perspective to write them down.

Lila saw movement from the corner of her eye. Someone else was on deck. Whoever it was didn't speak to her. She felt a surge of camaraderie toward the unknown person for leaving her alone. After a while, she placed her pen in the journal and set it down. She wrapped her arms around her knees and stared out at the water, letting her thoughts drift.

The other figure, on a chaise, stood and approached. The hair on the back of her arms prickled, and she didn't need to look to know it was Jackson.

"Hi," he said.

She wondered how someone could make one simple word sound so seductive. It couldn't be just the Southern drawl. "Hi back." Lila kept her eyes on the river. It was easier to stay detached if she didn't look at him.

"You found Encantadora's best-kept secret."

She broke down and peeked at him. He was focused on a spot across the river. He held a stack of half-opened mail, but he looked as if his mind was miles away. *Why couldn't he be short and loud like Ryan? Or obnoxious like Guy? Why did he have to seem like such a nice guy?* Lila tried to remember if Brody had started out as a nice guy, but she couldn't quite muster an image of him to hold up against Jackson for comparison. They might as well be different species. Besides, Brody was beginning to feel like a long time ago.

"I see the sunburn is already healing." Jackson's voice was peaceful, like the final rays of sun dipping under the surface of the river.

"It feels better. Thanks for the aloe." She tried to keep her eyes off the lean muscles of his thighs and calves as he lowered himself onto the chaise next to her.

"It's the least I could do after the ridiculous scene I made last night. I don't know what I was thinking. I have no excuse."

"None?" Lila asked. *Guys like him always had some ready excuse.*

"None."

"Hmm." Lila was starting to feel disoriented by his proximity.

Jackson cocked an eyebrow, and the corner of his lip inched up. "You don't believe me?"

Lila averted her eyes from his charming, lopsided grin. Natural charm in a man should set off bells in her head, but with Jackson she got only a pleasant hum. It was terrifying. "I've been writing down some of my recent thoughts. Some things are becoming clearer to me."

"You keep a journal?" he asked, interested.

Lila steeled herself against his charm and forced her thoughts on what she'd written about Jenna's obsession with Jackson. "It's just a theory . . . but I think you're this good-looking, great-at-everything guy who's used to everything going his way."

To Lila's surprise, Jackson winced. Brody might have gloated over the same declaration.

"No doubt you're used to attention from girls. When I didn't fawn all over you, maybe you took it as a challenge. Then when you saw me with Joshua, your ego snapped. I don't blame you. You've probably been conditioned by people like Traci and Jenna."

Jackson didn't speak for a minute. He looked to be battling between berating and defending himself.

Lila pressed on before her resolve crumbled and she *did* end up fawning all over him. "I could add it's a pattern for you, but I haven't known you for long."

Jackson's demeanor slipped into nonchalance. "We clearly need to get to know each other better," he drawled.

Lila marveled at how he could be so relaxed. Brody would've been hopping mad by now. Maybe Jackson just didn't care, or he was good at accepting the truth.

"I'm not falling into that trap." She hoped she looked nonchalant too, because her heart was racing so fast she worried he'd hear it over Beethoven's Fifth.

Lila got the impression he wasn't buying her act. His lips kept twitching as he watched her.

She tried another tactic. "If you want a real challenge, you could go after someone like Regina. She's ornery."

"*You're* sort of ornery," he said, studying her.

Lila opened her mouth to respond, but Ryan and Lacey diverted her. They jumped up on deck from the path behind the restaurant.

"Dude." Ryan slapped Jackson's shoulder by way of greeting.

"Hey, Lila," Lacey said. "A bunch of us who finally got out of Twilight duty decided to hit one of the local crab shanties for drinks and dancing tonight. Want to join us?"

"Thanks, but I don't think—"

"C'mon, babe." Ryan didn't wait for her to finish. "You don't want to be stuck around this place—all the geezers are going to be hitting on you."

Lila winced. "How're you getting out of nightclub duty?"

Lacey answered. "We invited a small group of guests to join us so no one can complain we aren't entertaining them. Please come. It'll be fun. Besides, I don't want to be the only bad dancer there."

"I think I'd rather stay," Lila said.

"It's not like you'll get to go to bed early if you stay behind. I hear Patrick's looking to practice a few more numbers with you."

"Patrick?" Jackson asked.

Lila groaned. "I have to replace Regina in the show."

Jackson almost smiled at her. "*You're* going to dance as the Dark Witch?"

"Yes. So whatever you do with those ropes, you'd better not drop me."

"I'm not going to drop you. Next rehearsal isn't until Wednesday. Why would Patrick be looking for you tonight?"

Lila felt her cheeks go red. "I don't think he was impressed with my moves today. I have a feeling he's setting up remedial practice sessions."

Lacey piped in. "Then you'd better avoid Patrick at all costs.

He'll have you up until midnight leaping over mystical sleeping logs."

Lila cringed. She knew Lacey wasn't exaggerating. "I guess I'll go."

"Dude, you have to go too," Ryan told Jackson.

Lacey grabbed Lila's arm and gave a squeeze.

"You can count on it," Jackson said, not taking his eyes off Lila.

"*Please* give me something low-key tonight," Lila pleaded to Sophie at the restaurant. "A table without single guys would be nice."

Sophie looked as if Lila had spoken a foreign language, but she smiled and led Lila and the married couple behind her to a nice table near the dessert buffet. Two other couples and a girl who looked about eleven were already seated. Sophie had chosen well; the conversation revolved around children. One woman was going on about how much she loved the kids' facilities at the resort when Joshua and Jonathan appeared. Lila pulled back in her chair to talk to them.

"Miss Lila! Look. I ate all my dinner, and Daddy said I could have dessert. My dessert had a treasure box in it!" Jonathan held up a plastic toy covered in chocolate mousse.

"Hi there, Jonathan. Wow, that looks so cool! What was in the box?" Lila asked.

"Bubblegum, but I eated it." Jonathan leaned in to give Lila a kiss and patted her arm with a sticky hand. "Bye, Miss Lila. I love you." He turned to skip around the table.

"Hold up, Jonathan," Joshua said. "You got chocolate all over Miss Lila's things." He looked at the black-and-white book on the table and took the empty chair next to her. "It looks like I might have to replace this—it's been slimed."

"That's okay. It's just my journal. Everything in it's a rough draft anyway."

"This is the infamous journal?" Joshua asked, pretending to

weigh it in his hand. "Your life must be pretty interesting for it to be this heavy."

"Not very interesting," Lila said. "Mostly it's a bunch of quotations."

"Like words of inspiration?" He cast a glance over his shoulder at Jonathan, who was showing his treasure to a boy at the adjacent table. Joshua poured himself a hefty measure of wine and topped Lila's glass off too.

"Sort of. Quirky little sayings pop into my head when I'm stressed. I mix well-known sayings with my own adages. They're kind of corny, but they comfort me somehow," Lila tried to explain.

"Do people still say that?" Joshua smiled, catching Jonathan by the arm on his third loop around the table and giving him a settle-down-or-else look.

"People as corny as I am do." Lila grinned.

"Mind if I take a peek?"

"They're sort of embarrassing."

"More embarrassing than tripping into that girl with the . . ." He made a gesture like holding melons in front of his chest. ". . . on the boat and winding up with a nose full of feathers?"

Lila threw back her head and laughed. "That *was* pretty funny. It's a good thing Traci had a life jacket on—you might have poked out an eye."

"It's a good thing it wasn't one of the married men on board, or that tennis instructor would be busy right about now."

Lila gave him a blank stare.

"Drew. The lawyer?" Joshua prompted. "See, I have a valid reason for checking into this journal. I need to make sure you haven't captured any blackmail material on me."

Lila clamped her hand to her chest. "*Moi?* Okay . . . but promise not to laugh."

Joshua traced an *X* over his heart and flipped open the cover. Lila held her breath, feeling like her soul had been exposed.

After a few minutes, Joshua snorted. "These are great. Seriously, you do this just for fun?"

"And therapy."

He read through another column, then looked up at Lila, a glimmer in his eye. "I'm forming an idea."

"Bonfire?" Lila said.

"Hardly. You know, I own a Chinese restaurant in SoHo, and I'm always looking for ways to create a unique experience for the customers. What do you think about letting me make some of your sayings into fortune cookies?"

Lila stared at him, blinking. Had he just said he wanted to buy her writing? As in, *pay* for something she'd written? "You . . . have a *Chinese* restaurant in *SoHo?*"

Joshua laughed. "Yes. I get that a lot—but business is good. What do you think? I could pay you about"—he rolled his eyes toward the ceiling as if making a quick calculation—"two dollars a fortune. I'll take what you've already got here. If they take off, maybe we can work out something more lucrative."

Four hundred dollars? It wasn't the mother lode, but for a bunch of random sayings that rattled around in her head twenty-four seven? "Seriously?"

"You need to check with an agent or someone?" Joshua asked, serious.

Lila laughed. "I wish. You have a deal."

Joshua raised his wine glass. Lila gave it a clink with her water glass and took a victorious sip.

Chapter Eleven

J ackson watched Lila raise her glass in a toast. *Unbelievable.*
Using his kid to hit on her. Did Lila really think that guy wanted
anything more than a week's entertainment? She looked so
damn happy. Vulnerable and happy. Jackson shook his head.
Sure, she's happy now, but what about after he goes back to the
real world and she's stuck here nursing . . . what? A broken
heart? A spear of envy shot through him. How could she let
herself get attached to some guy just passing through? He'd
watched scenes like these unfold many times. *Lila doesn't under-*
stand the way this place works. Having a kid only gives Joshua
the impression of being safe, and he is playing it up big time.

Jackson kept his eyes glued to Lila's table until Joshua and his
son left. Lila stayed another ten minutes, chatting with a couple.
Jackson wondered if Joshua had arranged to meet her somewhere after he put the kid to bed. The thought sent a pain knifing
through Jackson's chest. At least he knew Lila's immediate plans
involved her peers at the Crab Shanty tonight. It's a good thing
Ryan had thought to invite him, or Jackson would've had to pretend to be interested in one of the guests to tag along.

"Penny for your thoughts, handsome," Pascalle said. She

72

slipped into the chair next to him and followed his line of sight to Lila. "She's sweet."

"Who?" Jackson sounded surly and jealous, even to his own ears.

"You've been staring at Lila all night."

Jackson peeled his gaze away and twisted the stem of his wineglass.

"Don't bother denying it. Even Jenna has noticed. Lila will be lucky if she doesn't end up with Twilight duty every night for the rest of the season. Jenna makes up the schedules, you know."

Jackson looked at Pascalle. He'd never taken the time to get to know her, but she was okay. At least she'd never thrown herself at him, and she seemed pretty serious with Drew.

"She might be better off," he said.

"Better off locked up in Twilight all season?" Pascalle was surprised. "Better for whom?"

Jackson shrugged.

"You like her."

Jackson turned the full force of his gaze on her, and Pascalle flinched. He'd have to watch that. "I just don't like to see anyone get taken advantage of."

"Whatever you say. Jenna will be glad, at any rate."

"A wet *what* contest?" Lila asked, even though she'd heard.

"T-shirt. It'll be fun!" Lacey yelled to be heard over the rowdy music. "If we win, we get free drinks."

"Just what you need, free drinks." Lacey already had to hang on to the bar top to keep from falling over.

"Not just tonight. Every Friday for the month!"

"Lacey, how many more Fridays this month do you suppose you'll get off duty from the resort? Besides, look around you. There's no shortage of takers to buy you a drink if you want one."

Case in point, a lanky guy with too many freckles meandered up to Lacey. "Can I buy you a drink?"

"Sure!" Lacey said. "But only if you convince my friend here to join the wet T-shirt contest."

The guy's face lit up. "Sounds like a good idea to me."

Lila rolled her eyes. "What a surprise."

"Tell you what," he said. "I'll buy you a drink whether you join the contest or not. They call me Generous Jim back home."

"No thanks. I'm not joining any contests," Lila said.

Tall Man leaned in toward Lacey. "She get the worm in her tequila?"

"No, Jimmy," Lacey said, "Lila's problem is that she's drinking club soda with lime, and she hates men. She's bordering on being a stick in the sand."

"I don't hate men." Lila stabbed at her lime with a straw.

"You do if they're good looking. I've noticed. And you're being a party pooper, Lila. You said you'd dance with me so I wouldn't have to make a fool of myself."

Lila watched Lacey sway into Generous Jim and thought about telling her she was too late, but Lila was starting to think of Lacey as a friend. She didn't want to alienate her. "Okay. I'm sorry I'm being a stick in the mud. I'm not joining any contest, but I *will* dance."

Lacey jumped up and down, clapping her hands in delight. "Hooray, Lila! Let's go."

"Not yet." Lila eyed the dance floor of bodies, then Jim. "I think I may like a drink first."

Jackson watched Lila, one arm draped around Lacey and the other around a tall guy at the bar. They moved back and forth to Jimmy Buffet's "Margaritaville." Jackson counted the fruity drink she had been nursing as her first, so he figured she was a lightweight. That meant it'd be too easy for someone to take advantage of her. Jackson watched her tuck the colorful umbrella her drink had come with behind her ear, and he frowned. *Why am I bothering?* It wasn't like he owed her, and she didn't remind him of a sister or anything—in fact, far from it. He was beginning to think Pascalle was right. He had more than just a little thing for Lila. He liked her. *Really* liked her.

Lila didn't notice when her purse slid off her lap and got caught between the posts of the barstool. The music picked up a livelier beat, and the girl sitting across from Jackson asked if he wanted to dance. He slid his eyes back to Lila. She was making her way to the dance floor.

"Yeah, sure."

Ryan gave him a high five, and the girl bounced on her heels. Jackson reminded himself to keep some body distance between them on the dance floor.

Keeping distance proved impossible. Bodies were packed in so closely they meshed with every beat. The fact irritated Jackson as he watched Lila get tossed like an empty bottle in a rough ocean. He had trouble keeping track of her. When his dance partner wrapped her arms around his neck, he made a point of peeling them away and yelling in her ear that he was going to sit the next one out. Her disappointment melted when he steered her toward a buff guy in sandals who'd just started a line dance behind her. Jackson wove through the crowd, planting himself near Lila's abandoned barstool, now occupied by some guy with a bad sunburn.

Lila and Lacey cut through the crowd. "I'm so thirsty!" Lila called over the tempo, her cheeks flushed pink. She reached for the drink she'd left at the bar.

Jackson stretched and slipped his hand over the rim before she could pick it up. "You're not planning to drink that." He hoped his tone left no room for argument.

"I wasn't planning to swim in it." Lila furrowed her brow, trying to pry his fingers away.

"You've been gone for three dances. Anyone could've slipped something into your drink, and you'd never know. Never finish an unattended drink."

Lila gawked at him. "Thanks, but my drink doesn't need a chaperone."

"Maybe *you* do," Jackson said.

Lacey, standing on Lila's other side, half-leaning on the tall man, cut in, "Maybe *you're* just being a party stick in the pooper." Her eyes went wide. "Did I just say what I just heard?"

Lila raised her eyebrows at Jackson. "Well, if the *stick fits*."

Lacey held her stomach and doubled over from laughing before turning pale. "Oh. I don't feel so good."

Tall Man piped in. "I'll take you home."

Jackson placed a firm hand on his shoulder, though he had to reach up to do it. "No, you won't, cowboy."

"I'll take her." Ryan joined the little group, shaking his head at Jackson. "After you dumped Alicia, her friend dumped me. Thanks a lot, dude."

Jackson shrugged.

"The least you can do is teach me your backward water-ski move."

"I'm not—"

"I know; you're not a water-ski instructor. You still owe me." He coaxed Lacey out the back door for some fresh air.

The tall man watched her go with a glum expression, then turned to Lila. "Drink?"

"I don't think so," Jackson said.

"Waste of thirty bucks," the guy muttered before being swallowed by the crowd on the dance floor.

Lila swiveled to face Jackson, bubbling with indignity. "You don't own me."

"But I *am* your friend, and I'd like to get you in a cab before you wind up sand-wrestling some jerk who doesn't know the meaning of the word *no*."

Lila watched Jackson retrieve her purse from under the barstool. *How'd it get there?* He circled his fingers around her upper arm and nudged her away from the bar. The blood capsules under her skin started to zing. Outside, Lila took a deep breath of salty-sweet night air, and her mind flew to the memory of Jackson's kiss. That, combined with the realization that she was alone with Jackson, set off warning sirens in her head.

"No," she said.

Jackson's eyes raked the boulevard for a taxi. Lila searched the street too, but she found no headlights. Probably most cabs didn't show up until closer to last call.

"We need to go back inside to call a cab," Jackson said.

"No," Lila repeated.

Jackson ignored her. He eased her up the plank leading back to the bar. Lila ground her heels into the soft wood.

"Look who doesn't know the meaning of *no*," she said through gritted teeth.

Jackson stopped and looked at her. "What?"

"I said I don't want to go back with you. I . . . I don't want to be alone with you." She bit down hard as soon as the words were out.

Jackson looked surprised and a little insulted. "You don't have to worry about me. I won't take advantage of you when you've been drinking."

"I barely had one drink!"

"You don't have to worry about me," he repeated.

Lila snorted. "Convincing words from someone with a new girl in his lap every minute."

Jackson lost what was left of his temper. He leaned in close enough for her to feel hot breath on her cheek. The sensation raised the hair on her arms. "Lacey and Ryan are gone. I'm not leaving you here alone, and since cabs are scarce, you're coming back with *me*."

No way, no how am I leaving with you, sweet-talking Jackson from Georgia. "I'll walk."

Jackson looked at her like she'd suggested a swim home.

"I was paying attention when we drove here," Lila said. "It's less than two miles to the resort if I follow the main road."

"You're going to walk?"

"I'll start now." She took a few tentative steps, then strode in the direction of the resort.

Not far from the lights of the bar, the temperature dropped. Inky shadows loomed around her. Her strappy sandals slipped and crunched on the gravel covering the shoulder of the road. Lila strained her ears for Jackson's footsteps behind her, but she didn't pause to listen, in case he'd see her hesitation. *I won't look back.* She jumped at something that rustled in the overgrowth to her left. A lizard darted across the road into the blackness on the other side.

What was I thinking, again? Walking back had seemed like a great idea with Jackson hanging around too close for comfort, but now . . .

Stop your wishful thinking, Lila. You don't trust him.

Maybe the truth is you don't trust yourself, a voice inside countered. *You have a history of making bad choices with men.*

The fact that she found Jackson irresistible the more she knew him wasn't his fault. But with Brody fresh in her mind, it was a red flag to run.

Then again, Jackson had been caring tonight . . .

Strike that thought. That's just how his kind operated. Hadn't Brody seemed sincere before he trampled her trust? She wouldn't go through that again. One more semester, then she'd focus on her career. With Joshua's help, she might even have a jump start.

The sound of moving grass and something bigger than a lizard cut into Lila's thoughts. She'd forgotten all about alligators. Hadn't she heard somewhere that they hunted at night? She tried to remember how fast they could run. Faster than her, for sure. *This was a very bad idea.*

"Lila," Jackson's voice called from the black curtain behind her.

"Jackson?"

"For a girl afraid of predators, this wasn't such a bright idea."

She turned around to find the outline of his broad shoulders not too far behind. She'd thought he looked good earlier; now he looked downright wonderful.

Lila abandoned all pretense of bravery as she thought of what might be lurking in the grass. "I'm beginning to agree with you." As Jackson neared, she was tempted to launch into his arms and let him carry her, but even she couldn't stand the hypocrisy after she'd accused him of being a player. She opted to walk close to his side. He radiated a comforting heat. Still, she kept her ears alert for the pitter-patter of reptilian feet.

They walked in silence a few minutes before Jackson cast her a sideways look. "What's your story, Lila? Why are you here?"

"Poor judgment," Lila said. "Should have waited for the cab."

"I don't mean *here,* here. I mean at the resort. You don't seem the type."

Lila bristled and picked up her pace. "I'm doing the best I can. Maybe I'm not Traci or—"

Jackson took her hand and pulled her to a stop, facing her. "Why are you bent on twisting everything I say?"

His hand around hers heated the blood pulsing in her fingertips. She faltered. "I . . . I'm not."

"I've watched you work. You're good at your job, no question. What I meant is you're *different,* Lila. You seem out of your skin with any attention other than from the kids. You have to admit, it's unusual. More than half the people here are egomaniacs."

Lila shrugged. She couldn't argue with him. She would play her part to fulfill her bargain with Cliff, but she wasn't going to change to please anyone. Not even Jackson Koble. She pulled her hand away and stared ahead. "I can't help who I am."

Jackson's voice softened. "I like who you are. I just can't figure you out."

Lila's eyes snapped to his face. That was unexpected.

Jackson squinted into the distance as if looking for the answer. "I'm all for a change of scenery at the opportune time, Lila, but don't do anything you'll regret just to cover up a painful memory. They have a nasty habit of burrowing deeper the harder you try to uproot them."

Lila's jaw dropped. She hadn't shared her feelings with anyone. How could he hit so close to the mark? Unless . . .

"Sounds like you're speaking from experience," she said carefully.

He met her gaze. "I live my life with my eyes wide open. Don't pretend to be something you're not. I don't like to see good people get hurt." He started walking again.

Lila stood there, feeling exposed. He thought she was a good person? Even after she'd been so standoffish? He wasn't asking her for anything, but couldn't it all be a game to him?

"You coming?" he called over his shoulder.

Lila rushed to catch up. She tried to keep some space between them, but a host of nighttime noises still stalked them, and she stayed glued to his side. A couple of times, she almost grabbed his hand before thinking better of it.

Jackson shook his head and grinned into the darkness. "I swear, I've never met a more stubborn woman." He thought about it a minute. "Well, not one that I don't think of as a sister, anyway."

"You think of me like a sister?" Lila asked hopefully.

"Nope." Jackson laughed.

"A cousin?"

"Uh-uh."

"Like a friend?"

Encantadora's lights came into view. Jackson picked up his pace. "Not quite," he said. "But you're getting closer."

Chapter Twelve

TRUST YOUR INTUITION;
THEN TAKE OUT INSURANCE.
LUCKY NUMBERS: 3 7 14 21 23 9

The next days passed with increasing gratification. The resort was starting to feel less like a tight shoe Lila'd been squeezed into and more like a temporary home. She still had her long-term plans to keep in mind, though. She wanted to piece together a short story during her free time, in addition to the anecdotes for Joshua. It wouldn't do to return to Arizona with rusty writing habits.

To return. The thought held less appeal than it had a few days ago.

Regina's quarantine to the infirmary meant one fewer roommate to contend with. Even the weather had cooperated to lure her in. It was less humid, with clear skies, and tropical flowers filled the air with a cornucopia of pleasing aromas. Then there was Jackson. His boat tour had become so popular, they'd added a sunset-and-twilight tour, keeping him busier than usual. Whether she wanted to or not, Lila was able to avoid him, except for show rehearsals. At those, he spent most of the time in the rafters. That didn't keep her from being aware of him. He was the muscle at the end of the ropes that kept her on her toes and, truth be told, from falling flat on her face. Lila even found herself enjoying her role in *That Wizard of Ours*. She knew she'd miss the kids when the week ended. Jonathan, especially.

"How many sleeps left?" Jonathan asked for the fifth time since lunch. He'd paused from digging a moat for his sand castle and squinted through the sun at Lila.

"Just one more, sweetie. But don't worry; I'm going to be in touch with your daddy often, and I'll be sure to write to you too." She tugged down the rim of his hat to shade his eyes. "Maybe I'll even send a little reminder of me, like some shells or a bottle of sand."

Jonathan pondered that. "The girls' bathroom remembers me of you. You made me feel better."

Lila laughed, then poured a handful of sunscreen for a little girl whose shoulders had started to turn pink.

"Is my daddy going to marry you?" Jonathan asked.

"Oh." Startled, Lila dropped the sunscreen bottle in the sand. She picked it up and wiped sand from the rim. "No, Jonathan. Your daddy and I are just friends."

"Good friends? Like my mommy was with the delivery man?"

"Um. Probably not quite like that," Lila guessed, chewing her bottom lip.

Jonathan thought for a minute. "I guess that's okay. Will you come to visit?"

"Maybe I'll get to New York someday, but in the meantime, you'd better write to me. I'm counting on it."

"I only know how to write my name." Jonathan's tiny forehead creased.

"Then you can draw me a picture and write your name underneath it."

Jonathan nodded before resuming work on his sand structure.

Lila peered across the river toward the lush green on the other side that hid a channel leading to the ocean. Jackson had his boat out again, for the afternoon river excursion. Against her will, excitement brewed for the next time she'd get to take Little Delights on his tour. Unfortunately, that wasn't until next Tuesday. Jackson not only captained the river tours and headlined the water-ski show, but he also occasionally gave private sailing lessons and, more rarely, headed deep-sea-fishing excursions.

Lila couldn't help admiring Jackson's natural water talents and how easily he related to everyone. She was less thrilled with her overall admiration of him, which, ironically, became harder to ignore the more time she spent away from him. She'd taken to brooding about Brody and the wrongs he had done to her just to remember why an attraction to Jackson was a bad idea.

"Time to shake down, Little Monkeys!" Ryan called from his perch on a boulder near the river path. "On your feet and shake-shake-shake the sand from your pants!"

The kids jiggled their heads and bodies. Sand streamed from the little folds in their clothing and from their hair.

"Good! Keep that skip in your step, because after a snack we're going to have our last practice for the big Jungle Show tonight. Are you ready?"

"Yeah," a dozen keyed-up voices called.

"Awesome!" He turned to Lila. "Miss Lila, pick up the caboose, and off we go. Repeat after me, Monkeys: Ooo-ooo-ooo!"

Lila grinned at Ryan. His heart was in the right place. Maybe acting like a kid was the secret to success.

"Now show me a lion: Rrrrroar!" He scrunched up his face like a ferocious beast and fake-swiped her with a claw, then winked. "Oops, pretend you didn't see that. I don't want it getting back to Jackson, or I'll never get those skiing tips."

Lila's mouth fell agape, but before she could question him, he took off with the front of the Party Train.

The Jungle Show went off without a hitch. The little kids had been subdued by being on stage in front of hundreds of eyes, so they were easier to control. The older kids managed to remember most of their steps. What they missed, no one noticed. They received thundering applause and a standing ovation.

Joshua joined Jonathan backstage, crushing him with a hug. "Awesome job, little man! For a minute I thought you were a *real* lion." Jonathan's face glowed. Joshua turned to Lila. "I guess this is it. We've got an early flight in the morning, so we're leaving right before dawn."

Lila looked at Jonathan, hugging her leg. He rubbed his face and smeared the black paint on his nose from ear to ear. Lila blinked away the tears. "I'm going to miss you guys." She ruffled Jonathan's hair.

Joshua kissed her on the cheek. "I'll shoot you an e-mail and let you know how the fortunes are going, but either way, I'm expecting to hear from you in April. Don't make me get back on a plane and come down here." He smiled.

Lila nodded. Who knew saying good-bye after one week could be so hard?

Joshua gave her a kiss on the other cheek. "See you, kiddo." He scooped up Jonathan before the little guy realized what was happening and told him to say good-bye. Jonathan waved as Joshua started walking away.

As Lila watched them retreat through watery eyes, she became aware of Jackson. He stood in a corner backstage, holding out pen and paper to a group of jungle animals, asking for autographs. A dozen little figures in furry costumes crushed against him, giggling in delight. His eyes flicked over their heads and met Lila's. His face became serious for a moment as he studied her, maybe wondering at the tears. Then his gaze followed Joshua and Jonathan before he dropped it back to the kids thronging him.

Lila felt a pang of affection, then pushed it away. So what if Jackson was incredible with children? It didn't make him less of a player. She watched a girl dressed like an elephant sign his notepad. Her stuffed trunk bopped him under the chin every time she looked up, but Jackson only laughed. Lila felt her stomach clench. She was weakening. She'd have to do something soon, or she'd end up right where she started.

She scanned the room for Joshua and Jonathan, who'd almost made it to the door. This could be her one chance to drive Jackson away for good. On impulse, she rushed forward to grab Joshua by the elbow, then placed a hand on either side of his face. She planted her sealed lips smack atop his and held the position for a long while before pulling away. Joshua blinked at her, wide-eyed and chagrined. She gave him an apologetic smile and whispered that she'd explain when she wrote to him later. When she turned back, Jackson was gone.

Success.

A feeling of loss washed over her as Joshua and Jonathan, too, ebbed into the crowd. *I did it.* She scanned the room of carefree strangers. *So why don't I feel like celebrating?*

Lila was grateful to see Jenna engaged in a phone conversation when she approached the front desk. Bertrand was stuffing itineraries into Tour Paradise envelopes. He looked up from the task when Lila approached.

"Hello there. What can I do for *you?*"

"Can you tell me where the nearest bank is?" Lila asked.

Bertrand leaned across the desk, resting his chin between two fingers. "What's it worth to you?"

"$354.38." Lila waved the envelope containing the net sum of her first paycheck.

"I didn't mean in cash," Bertrand said, waggling his eyebrows at her.

"Good, because I'm squirreling away every penny to finish school."

Bertrand eyed the check. "Looks like you'll be squirreling for a long time."

Lila sighed. The reality of the paycheck she'd get each week did nothing to buoy her spirits, but there were guests lounging in the white wicker furniture behind her, so she kept smiling. "Where can I cash it?"

Bertrand pulled a map from beneath the counter and circled

the nearby banks with a felt-tip pen. From the corner of her eye, Lila noticed Jackson enter the open reception area, chatting with the guests behind her. She tilted her head so she could see him better, and he chose that moment to look her way. His face went blank as he turned away. Lila dismally congratulated herself again. *Not so much as a hello.*

Jenna hung up the phone and scowled at Lila.

Bertrand waved his marker in front of her. "Hello? Paradise to Lila. Did you hear what I said?"

"Sorry, no."

"If you open an account at Florida Mutual, you get a free lunch cooler."

"Thanks, but I don't plan on opening an account. I just need to cash the check."

"Want to keep the money handy in case you need to bolt, huh?"

"Something like that." Lila eyed the check. It wasn't much, but without room and board to pay for, she could save it all. Pleased by the prospect of taking a baby step toward replacing the funds Brody had pilfered, Lila gave Bertrand a genuine smile before turning to claim one of the waiting taxis.

Jackson overheard part of Bertrand's conversation with Lila, and he didn't like it. What reason would she have to bolt? She'd just gotten there. She must've been more upset by losing Joshua than he realized. He watched her cab take off, and his heart constricted. He approached the front desk and waited for a break in Jenna and Bertrand's conversation.

"She's not depositing it?" Jenna asked Bertrand.

Bertrand shrugged. "Guess not."

"She's planning to keep cash in her room safe? Even though it's shared with all her roommates?"

"So?" Bertrand asked.

"It's just very trusting, that's all."

"Any messages?" Jackson asked.

Jenna jumped at his voice, but she composed herself, flashing a practiced smile.

Jackson looked at Bertrand.

"Your box is stuffed with them. Someone named Manny." Bertrand handed him a fistful of messages.

Jackson leaned against the counter to read them. Five were from Manny. He had stalled the seller in Puerto Rico, but now the man wanted an answer by next Friday or he'd write off Cast-a-Line and sell to another buyer. Jackson ran his hand through his hair. Who would run the business if he expanded, anyway? These days, Cast-a-Line needed every hand on deck just to keep the flagship office running. If Jackson gave up the idea of expansion, his father would have understood. Wouldn't he have?

Jackson thought about the planning sessions he'd had with his father. *We're on the map, son. Tybee's successful. Now's the time to cast a line across new waters. Your son and his son's sons will have a piece of paradise across the globe to call their own.* An ache flooded Jackson's chest. It was unfair. His father, who'd been close to fulfilling his dream, had been cheated. Jackson may not care about expanding, but Old Kobie had wanted it. He'd wanted it for the two of them and for their future.

The sense of responsibility Jackson had been suppressing flared. He didn't relish the thought of buying some ready-made commercial tour company, but he knew he'd have to check the place out. He doubted it would have the same *essence,* as his father put it, as the Tybee place. Still, there was more than enough money to give his father's dream a chance.

Jackson thumbed through the rest of the messages, all from Pug. The first said she was on her way to Vegas. The second told him she and Fish had been married without a glitch and were off to the honeymoon. She'd *Gone Fishing.* She'd even made Bertrand write *wink-wink.* Jackson reread the message and grinned. "Bertrand, is there any way you can have flowers and a pound of Swedish Fish sent to someone for me?" He scrawled a message of congratulations on a slip of paper.

"Sure. How much do you want to spend on the flowers?" Bertrand asked.

"Whatever it takes for two dozen tiger lilies."

Jenna piped in. "I *love* tiger lilies. Who're they for? Your mother?"

"My mother passed on years ago," Jackson said without looking at her. He handed Bertrand the message and the address from Pug's message along with two hundred-dollar bills. "Let me know if that doesn't cover it."

"I'm sorry, Jackson," Jenna said, attempting to place a hand on Jackson's shoulder.

"Forget about it, Jenna," he said as he walked away.

Jenna stuck out her lower lip. "That's so sad. I remember someone saying his dad died recently, too. I'll bet he doesn't have a soul to rely on, poor guy. He's broke and stuck in a go-nowhere job—"

"Hey," Bertrand said. "*We're* in this job."

"*We* have an education and work in the office. *He* comes from some backwater island in Georgia and drives an old boat. Don't get me wrong. With his looks and talent, it makes no difference to me if he's penniless."

"Considering he just handed me two hundred dollars for flowers and candy, I doubt he's penniless." Bertrand fingered the cash Jackson had folded into the message.

Jenna frowned. "Who are the flowers for?" She reached out to snatch the paper, but Bertrand pulled away.

"No you don't. Even around here, there's a little thing called privacy. It's rare, but it exists."

Jenna scowled and turned back toward her work. In her peripheral vision she saw Bertrand tuck the message into his shirt pocket. She eyed the cubbies along the back wall that served as mailboxes. Jackson's was empty now, but Lila's spilled over. She hadn't asked for her messages earlier.

When Bertrand moved to answer the phone, Jenna snagged Lila's messages and tucked them in the waistband of her shorts. When she'd locked herself into the bathroom stalls, she saw they all came from some guy named Brody. She stared at the back of the yellow bathroom door and tried to piece the messages together. *Who is Brody and why is he so desperate to connect with Lila?* Jenna flushed all the messages save one down the toilet. Looks like she'd just have to find out.

Chapter Thirteen

Are you babes just going to sit up here all day and sunbathe?" Ryan asked. "Aren't you at least going to watch?"

"Watching amateur jocks play softball in eighty percent humidity is not my idea of a good time," Lacey said. "We rarely get time off during the day. We're using it to work on our tans. Lila needs to even out."

"Your loss." Ryan opened the door leading down from the rooftop lounge to the inside of the building housing the staff accommodations.

The roof offered a primo sunbathing spot, because none of the guests knew about it. It gave the overworked employees a chance to relax without having to be *on* for the guests. Lacey untied the strap of her bikini top and rolled over on her stomach. Lila knew she would always have tan lines herself. As long it didn't look like she'd just hoed a dozen acres of potatoes, she was okay with that.

"Where are they playing?" Lila secured a paper clip over her page and closed her journal, then tucked it into her beach bag.

"In the field south of the lap pool."

"Do the guests play?"

"They can, but most of last week's guests are leaving for home today, and the new ones are still arriving or getting acclimated. I don't bother unless I know Henri will be there, but now that he's back with Isabelle, we won't see him during free time for a while. Lucky Isabelle."

Lila yanked her hair into a ponytail. "Do all the guys play?"

Lacey propped on one elbow, holding her towel to her chest. "You're fishing, Lila. Who're you interested in?"

Lila flipped open the magazine Lacey had abandoned and buried her nose so Lacey couldn't read her face. "No one."

"Right. Who is it? I know a bunch of guys who'd be interested: Bertrand, Guy, Fritz . . ."

Lila hoped her horrified expression convinced Lacey she lacked interest in any of those prospects.

"Wait a minute." Lacey's face turned smug. "I know."

Lila's pulse spiked. "There's nothing to know."

"You have fine taste, at least." Lacey grinned.

"I don't know what you're talking about." Lila flipped the page, zeroing in on an ad for lip gloss.

"Sure. You're not like *any* of the girls who've thrown themselves at him. You've got superhuman resistance. Heck, I practically threw myself overboard on my first river tour hoping he'd dive in after me and give me mouth to mouth."

"I haven't the slightest idea what you're talking about."

"Have it your way. But if you do ever get anywhere with him, you're required to dish on every detail. I have to live vicariously through someone, and since Isabelle never surfaces for air—"

The door leading to the roof opened and shut. Neither Lacey nor Lila looked up to see who entered, but Lila shushed Lacey, lest they be overheard. A shadow blocked Lila's sun, then Guy pulled a weathered lawn chair next to Lila's and peered over her shoulder.

Lila moved the magazine higher.

"Lila, you have kept me at bay long enough. Will you join me tonight at dinner? I can arrange to take you somewhere special on the waterfront."

"I don't think so."

Lacey stifled a laugh and turned away.

"I think I understand."

Obviously not.

"You don't want to take advantage of my connections. You want to make a good impression while you are here—knowing Cliff must get a regular report on your performance. You wish to go back to your job in Scottsdale when you are finished here, yes?"

Lila's eyes met Guy's without wavering. *Seriously? He's playing that card?* Lila didn't trust herself to respond. If she wasn't rude, he couldn't report anything derogatory to Cliff.

"Lila, you are being stubborn. Don't you like me?"

"I don't know you."

"Precisely what I am trying to rectify. You are cruel to refuse me."

Lila didn't say anything. Guy sighed and walked to the edge of the building. Maybe he'd give up after all.

He turned back to her with a look of defeat. "Forget dinner. What about a drink?"

"No, thanks," Lila said.

"But it's very hot, and you look thirsty. One soda?"

Lila considered that. She'd made it clear she wasn't interested. So what was the harm in having one soda at the bar? She *was* thirsty—she'd forgotten to bring a water bottle and was baking under the sun. Maybe if she proved she didn't have anything against him *per se,* he wouldn't make things difficult for her when she tried to go back to Scottsdale. As head of PR, he could complicate things if he wanted.

Guy spread his hands palms up in front of him, as if to signify his good intentions.

"Okay. *One soda.*"

Lacey whipped her head around. "Are you sure you know what you're doing?"

"It's a soda. Want me to bring you one?" Lila asked.

Lacey peered at Guy, the picture of innocence in his linen shirt, arms spread wide. "No thanks." She shrugged and closed her eyes again against the sun.

"I am happy you've changed your mind." Guy didn't conceal his enthusiasm.

Maybe she'd been too icy before. If she'd known one drink was all it'd take to get him off her back, she'd have done it ages ago. She wriggled into her T-shirt and shorts and draped her beach bag over her shoulder. "See you in a few," she told Lacey. "Save my chair."

They exited downstairs and through the courtyard. The paths were deserted, given everyone was either enjoying the hours of privacy or the softball game. When they reached the path branching toward the resort center, Lila continued straight when Guy veered left.

He stared at her, mystified. "Where are you going?"

"To the bar. For the soda." Lila wondered if maybe he had attention deficit disorder.

Guy threw his head back and laughed.

"What?" Lila asked, annoyed.

"When I invited you for a drink, I meant from the mini-refrigerator in my room."

Lila stared at him. "You can't have a mini-refrigerator in your room."

"But I do. On my honor." He gave her a virtuous smile.

Lila weighed her options. If it had been a genuine misunderstanding—and by the way Guy had split his side laughing, she assumed it was—she'd look paranoid if she didn't accept. She *really* didn't want to accept, but it would look bad if she bailed out now. "I'd be more comfortable at the main bar."

"Yes, and they charge almost five dollars a soda. Why overpay when I'm stocked in my room?"

He had a point there. No one at Encantadora got paid much,

and although she suspected Guy earned more than most, it didn't make sense to throw money away. She understood what it was like to be on a budget. "Okay."

Guy tugged her sleeve, steering her left.

This is going to be one very quick drink, Lila promised herself.

Guy's room was situated near the guest rooms, bordering the golf course and recreation areas. They passed within yards of the softball game. Lila wished she'd accepted Ryan's invitation to watch.

"Do you want to watch the game? It sounds exciting," Lila asked hopefully.

Guy shook his head. "Sweaty jocks or a cool drink? No contest. Here we are." He stepped up to one of the back patios and pulled the sliding glass door open. A blast of cold air hit them head-on. Lila had to admit that it felt good. Guy held the room-darkening curtain aside and gestured for her to enter.

Lila hesitated, glancing behind her. No one was around, but the game wasn't too far away, either.

"You're nervous, Lila. It wounds me to think you don't trust me." Guy held his arm up in mock surrender.

Lila entered and her eyes adjusted to the room. It seemed innocuous enough, everything tidy and the bed made. To her relief, a mini-refrigerator hummed from the corner.

Guy flicked a light switch, then walked to the refrigerator and handed Lila a can of soda. Then he smiled, as if to say *I told you so*.

Lila allowed herself to relax a fraction. Guy grabbed a regular cola for himself and popped the lid. "Glass of ice?"

"Sure." It would take Guy out of the room for a minute, and that would be less time spent alone with him.

"Be right back." He vanished behind a partition she knew must lead to a walk-in closet and a bathroom, probably for a bucket for the ice.

Lila planned to ask to join him to the ice machine. Once outside, she would find an excuse to finish the drink in a public place. While Guy shuffled around the closet, Lila scanned the room. A collage of a sweet-looking brunet adorned the wall. "Who's this girl in your collage?" Lila called.

"Carrie. She left last season."

Perfect. Nothing like discussing an ex-girlfriend to keep things platonic. "She's pretty. I bet you miss her a lot."

"She was beautiful. I do miss her," Guy responded from behind the wall. "Lila, can you come here and help me, please?"

Lila congratulated herself on finding a way to deal with Guy. She set down the soda and headed toward Guy's voice. She rounded the corner and saw he'd set two cups on the bathroom counter. Guy was still deep in the closet. Lila reached for a cup but dropped it when Guy emerged wearing only a pair of bikini underwear.

Lila let out a startled scream and spun her head away from the sight. It didn't take long to absorb the magnitude of the situation. Guy pushed up against her, forcing her into a corner of the bathroom.

"Lila. I want you. I know you want me, too, or you would not have agreed to come with me."

"No! This is all a mistake." She clambered to free herself, but Guy was stronger and she couldn't get around him. He pinned her arms to her sides.

"You are shy. Don't worry, I'll take care of everything." He smothered her neck.

Lila shrank back, trapped. She tried to crush her heel on his toes or lift her knee, but she couldn't get enough leverage. Terror washed through her. She squeezed her eyes shut against the nightmare and opened her mouth for another scream. Maybe a guest still lingering in his room would hear her.

A crash sounded from the other room, and Jackson burst in, a baseball bat gripped under white knuckles. He shot Guy a murderous scowl.

Relief flooded Lila. The bat spun off to the side while Jackson pried Guy from Lila and buried his fist into him. Guy crumpled in two. Jackson threaded the fingers of his hands and landed another blow on the back of Guy's neck. Guy lay on the ground, hugging his knees. With what looked like tremendous self-control, Jackson unclenched his hands and bent to grab Guy's hair, their noses almost touching.

"If you ever so much as blink in Lila's direction, nothing will stop me from coming back here to finish the job." Jackson's jaw muscles strained. He released Guy, who dropped back into a fetal position.

Jackson's eyes fell to Lila. She had to hug her body to keep from launching into Jackson's arms.

"Are you hurt?" Jackson ran his eyes over her, as if assessing damaged parts.

Lila shook her head.

"Let's get out of here." Jackson led her by the hand through the bedroom.

The curtain was torn off its hooks, and the sliding door was jarred from its tracks. Lila wouldn't have been surprised to find it shattered to bits. She grabbed the bag with her journal, and they crossed into the bright sunlight outside.

"How did you know—?" she asked as Jackson hurried away from the rooms.

Jackson gave her hand a gentle squeeze, but he didn't look at her. Fury tightened his eyes. "I was in the batter's box when I saw you enter Guy's room. You looked . . . rigid . . . like you didn't want to be with him. I had to check it out, to make sure you were okay. When I heard you scream . . ." His voice dropped away, and he struggled to keep composure.

"I'm glad you did." Tears from suppressed tension and gratitude spilled over.

Jackson stopped and turned to her. "Lila," his voice was tender. "You should report him."

A wave of terror shook her. "I can't!"

Jackson looked stricken as he watched her emotions surface. "I can't begin to imagine how you feel, Lila. But what if he does that again, to somebody else?"

"It . . . was a misunderstanding."

Jackson's eyes flickered with disbelief. "I heard you tell him *no*."

"I agreed to go in there with him. He assumed it meant . . ." She winced.

"You told him *no*. *No* is *no*. End of story."

"That sounds like it should be my line." Lila almost smiled before the grimness crept back.

"That *was* your line."

"I can't report it." She couldn't afford to lose her job now, and who knew what kind of clout Guy had? Tustin might not believe her. "You burst in before anything bad happened, but he might have come to his senses." She didn't believe that. She started to cry again, this time in gulping sobs.

Jackson looked as though he had to bite through his tongue to keep from turning back and ripping Guy from limb to limb. "I'm sorry, Lila. We can talk about this later, when you're not so upset."

Without Jackson letting go of her hand, they headed back toward the center of the resort. A few guests were beginning to trickle in. Lila stopped.

"What is it, Lila?" Jackson asked.

Lila marveled at the sensitivity in his voice. Brody had never sounded that way. Not even when her favorite aunt had passed away. "I don't want to be seen like this. And I don't think I can go back to my room just yet. Regina's there."

Jackson paused to think. "If you want to get away for a bit, and if you're not too uncomfortable being around me, I can take you out on one of the boats." He tipped her chin to meet her eyes. "I promise you on my parents' graves, I won't hurt you."

Lila almost laughed. "You *saved* me. I trust you."

There it was. She hadn't planned to say it, but she knew the truth of it. Jackson wouldn't harm her, not like Guy had tried to, and, she was pretty sure, not like Brody had done. Jackson was different. He was someone she could count on. At least she hoped he was, because she was going to let him in someplace fragile.

Her heart.

Chapter Fourteen

YOUR PASSIONS WILL SWEEP YOU AWAY;
RELAX AND ENJOY THE RIDE.
LUCKY NUMBERS: 3 5 24 36 28 11

Jackson worked the sails, taking the boat downriver to the open ocean. His face was set in focused lines, but his smooth, easy movements betrayed that the work was second nature to him. Lila wondered if the feigned concentration was his way of giving her space to think. The thought warmed her. They advanced through the passageway from river to ocean and skimmed into open water atop the gentle waves.

Lila lifted her face to the salt spray and breathed deeply, feeling a familiar longing. This was how Jackson smelled, like the ocean. He tasted the same way, if she remembered right, and who could forget? Closing her eyes, she gave way to the sensation of the small craft bumping against the rippled sur face. Some of the stress of the afternoon dulled, like the edges of a broken glass tumbled smooth against the surf. Jackson lowered the sails until the boat drifted among the waves.

Lila opened her eyes. He sat at the opposite end, arms resting on his knees, sea green eyes watching her. They didn't speak for a few minutes until Lila tried to thank him.

"I . . ."

"Shh. Try to relax. I won't bother you." Jackson turned his head toward the sunset, purple and orange on the horizon.

Lila was overwhelmed with affection. She stood, unsteady against the rocking boat, and ambled toward him. He turned his attention on her, watching with cautious intensity. She closed the short distance and slipped down next to him, brushing her knee against his. She reached out to hold his head between her trembling palms, and she pressed her lips against his. It surprised her how quickly the tender kiss built into something that left her breathless.

At first, Jackson seemed too stunned to react, but as her kiss deepened, she felt his hands bury in her hair as he pulled her against him. She didn't resist. All noise ceased except the thrumming of her heart and the muted slap of waves against the boat. A raging thrill traveled through her.

Jackson's body tensed. A strangled sound escaped his throat, and he pulled his mouth away from Lila. He whispered against her hair. "Are you sure this is what you want?"

"Yes." She kissed his throat.

He pulled her up and probed her eyes. "You seemed pretty set against getting involved with me. This could be a stress reaction to what happened today."

Lila felt certain that her eyes reflected only honest affection, but for his sake, she spoke with certainty. "I've been lying to myself. I want to be with you."

Jackson dipped his head and took her mouth, sliding his arms around her.

Lila's hand moved across the fabric of his sun-bleached shirt, curling into his chest.

Jackson pulled away and held her at arm's length. "We can't do this." He sounded agonized.

Understanding dawned. What she'd initiated as innocent kissing, to open her heart to this man, was in danger of escalating into a whole lot more. He thought she wasn't ready for that, and he was right. Lila chastised herself for being so naive.

"I'm sorry." She cast her eyes around the deck to keep from looking at his face.

Jackson lifted her chin. "I'm not."

He kissed her on the forehead, lingering for a second, then straightened and turned away to work the sails, steering the catamaran back toward the crowded inlet.

That was too close. Jackson wanted Lila, but not on the rebound. He knew she'd regret it.

By the time their craft reached the river and started upstream, the warm effect of their earlier encounter was replaced by the cool of the evening air. It worked the magic of clearing Jackson's mind. He saw Lila shiver from her perch at the front of the boat, and he motioned for her to sit with him. His heart swelled when she nestled into the curve of his arm and shoulder.

"I'm not sure I should have let that happen," he said.

The edge of Lila's mouth curled up. "Nothing happened, remember?"

"You call that nothing? One kiss, and you had me unglued."

Lila stared at the wake left by the boat.

"You've had a rough day. I'm just saying I should've let you have more space."

Lila turned to smile at him. "I'm not sure you had a choice."

He remembered the tears when they'd left Guy's and felt a spear of loathing. "You were pretty shaken up."

"It had nothing to do with what happened on the boat."

Jackson felt a wave of relief. Maybe it hadn't just been the stress. "You're absolutely sure?"

"I'm absolutely sure."

Jackson hugged her to him. "I want this too. I've lost too many people I care about. I didn't think I could feel this way. There's something about you, Lila. I can't pinpoint it, but it draws me. We're almost back." He released her to maneuver the boat around the last few tight bends.

"Oh, no!" Lila shot up in a panic. "The show. We're *missing* the show. Patrick's going to kill us."

Jackson laughed and drew her back down, kissing the tip of

her nose. "Don't worry. I heard Regina has recovered enough to handle the show after all."

Lila looked at him, disbelieving. "When were they going to tell me?"

"Uh—I think Patrick planned to discuss it with you at dinner."

Lila considered that. "But what about you? Don't you need to work the ropes?"

"Regina is state champion in gymnastics. I was there mostly for backup. They'll make do without either of us."

Lila looked both relieved and put out.

Jackson kissed her again. "I wouldn't worry about it. Unless you had aspirations for the stage, I think you're better off. You might even avoid the shows altogether, if you're lucky."

"I was that bad?" Lila winced.

"I think you're amazing, but as the Dark Witch? Let's just say it's a stretch of character." Jackson held her smile for a moment, then became serious. "Are you going to be okay going back?"

Lila's eyes reflected calm. "I am now."

Jackson hugged her again. "I'm glad, but I don't know how I'm going to keep from throttling Guy. The way I feel about you, there's no way I'm going to forget what he did."

He's talking about feelings. How did this happen? If Lila were honest, she'd have to admit what she felt for Jackson transcended the physical too. She was perilously close to being in love. She didn't want to think about how vulnerable that made her. She reached for her beach bag, and the journal fell onto the deck. The envelope with her money slipped from between the pages. Jackson gathered them and tucked the envelope underneath the paper clip marking her page, then handed the book to Lila.

"Still journaling?"

She nodded.

"Think I'll make the evening edition?"

Lila flushed. "To be honest, it's no longer just a journal. I'm working on some material for Joshua."

Jackson's face fell into grim lines. "Joshua."

"He agreed to buy some of my anecdotes for his restaurant. He'd going to put them inside fortune cookies. It's not much money, but it's a step in the right direction."

"I'm sure Joshua was all too willing to accommodate."

"You sound jealous."

"I just don't want you chasing after some guy who might be leading you on for personal reasons."

Lila couldn't help but smile at the torment on Jackson's face. She didn't intend to let it stay there for long. "Jackson, Joshua isn't interested in . . . women."

As her words registered, his expression of annoyance faded to jubilation. "That's a different story." He jumped off the deck onto the pier with renewed vigor. He held out his hand for her.

"Right." Lila smiled to herself.

Most of the guests and staff were mingling at the main bar after the evening show, so she wouldn't have to worry about running into Guy right away. Jackson walked Lila to her room and waited while she threw her bag on her rumpled cot.

"You'll be all right alone?" he asked.

"The show's over. One of the girls will come along soon."

As if to make the point, Regina elbowed her way past Jackson and into the room. Jenna was close on her heels. Jenna stopped in the doorway and looked between Jackson and Lila, not hiding her annoyance at finding them together. "Regina, you're going to need to fill out an accident report," she said.

Regina slammed the door in her face. "Let *him* fill out the report." She eyed Jackson and Lila. "Sorry about that."

They stared at her. Lila couldn't remember Regina ever initiating a conversation, let alone apologizing for her behavior. "Was there an accident?" Lila asked.

Regina snorted. "None serious enough."

Jackson arched his eyebrows. "Want to talk about it?"

Regina shrugged. "Not much to tell. Guy came sniffing around earlier to talk to Lila."

Jackson stiffened and Lila saw the muscle in his jaw work, but he didn't comment.

"He made a major miscalculation and tried to bite me."

Lila's mouth dropped open.

"Idiot thought he'd give me a European greeting, but instead of kissing my cheek he nipped it. Like he could get away with biting *me*." She laughed.

Lila had a sudden flash of Regina as an effective Dark Witch. "So—you caused an accident?"

"I may have broken his wrist." Regina proceeded to throw laundry off her cot into a mesh bag. "He should be on his way to the hospital now. He may be walking sort of funny too."

"Ouch." Jackson winced, but his smile was broad now. "You're all right though?"

Regina rolled her eyes, then stopped sorting laundry. "What did Guy want with you, anyway?"

Lila stiffened.

"Okay, never mind." She looked from Lila to Jackson. "Whatever it was, I assume you're all right now?"

Lila looked at Jackson and nodded.

"But Guy isn't," Jackson said with smug satisfaction.

"Guy will be heading home straight after the hospital."

Lila was flabbergasted. "He was fired?"

Jackson didn't look as surprised. "Regina has some special influence over Tustin."

"You're *in couple* with Tustin?" Lila blurted. Talk about a well-kept secret.

"Okay, people. I'm recovering from strep throat, and this conversation is wearing on my vocal cords, not to mention my nerves. Can we call it a night?"

Lila bit her bottom lip to keep from smiling. Regina had a soft center after all. "Sure. We were just leaving."

"Actually"—Jackson looked at Lila with regret—"speaking of Tustin reminds me that I need to talk with him about something."

Lila let her eyes linger over her cot. "It's okay. I wouldn't mind making it an early night."

"You'll be okay?" He probed her as if checking for signs of lingering pain.

"Are you kidding?" She laughed. "I've got *Regina* at my back."

Tustin was wiping stage makeup from his face when Jackson joined him in the costume room backstage. He took in Jackson's faded T-shirt and beach shorts, and he gave a gruff laugh. "Dressed to the nines, as usual. I know I've been loose with the rules for you, Koble, but you'd better clean up good tomorrow night for Sunday formal."

"I always do," Jackson said. "Can I have a word?"

"Just one. My schedule's off course. I had to do the show at the last minute."

"I know. We ran into Regina."

Tustin looked only mildly surprised and didn't ask whom *we* referred to. One of the things Jackson liked best about Tustin was that he respected people's privacy.

"What is it?"

"I need another favor," Jackson said.

In spite of his casual demeanor, Tustin appeared nonplussed. "It's a good thing you're outstanding at your job, or you'd be out of work and forced to face those demons you're running from." His words were harsh, but Jackson appreciated the concern behind them. Tustin was a good guy. He eyed Jackson, waiting for a response.

"Those demons are why I'm here. They've come knocking, and this time they can't wait. I need a few days off to deal with them."

Tustin looked at him with part disbelief, part admiration. "You're going back, eh?"

"Not quite yet, but I need to take care of some things."

"You should go back," Tustin said.

Jackson nodded. "I know, but I can't yet. Still, I can't avoid making at least one decision."

"And after that?"

"I'm coming back here," Jackson said without wavering. "But after this season, I may decide to settle down."

"About time. Not that I can afford to lose you." He reached out and shook Jackson's hand. Tustin understood that Encantadora was a stopover for Jackson on his way to settling into his own burgeoning tour business. "I'd like to work something out, if you ever decide to set up shop in Florida."

"You bet. For now, I've got my hands full elsewhere. Okay if I leave Monday morning? I can be back in three days."

Tustin nodded. "You'll need to get someone to cover for you in the water-ski show. Think you can teach Bertrand or Ryan some of your moves in time?"

Jackson shook Tustin's hand. "I can try. Thanks."

He heard Tustin call out to him just before he shut the door to the dressing room. "What's her name, Koble?"

Jackson paused, looking back with a slow smile. "Is it that obvious?"

"Let's just say I know the feeling."

"Lila Hayes."

"The new girl from Scottsdale, eh? I should've known she'd take someone down. Cliff warned me she was something else."

Jackson felt his heart constrict. "She's something else, all right."

Chapter Fifteen

THE SIMPLEST ANSWER IS TO ACT;
THEN HOLD ON TIGHT AND HOPE FOR THE BEST.
LUCKY NUMBERS: 11 15 2 27 36 1

Lila watched from the restaurant's deck as Jackson pulled Ryan, and then Bertrand, behind the water-ski boat for the umpteenth time. They'd been skiing all morning and afternoon between boat tours. Lila and Lacey had been forced to pick up Ryan's slack in Little Delights. That hadn't left Lila with one free minute since breakfast. It was a good thing they had the six-to nine-year-old crowd this week, or they'd have never made do. As it was, Lila hadn't gotten to speak to Jackson since he'd left her room the prior night. She wondered what had convinced Jackson to share his water-ski tips with such sudden relish. Neither Ryan nor Bertrand had half of Jackson's talent, but they'd gotten the slalom jump down pat.

Lacey spoke over Lila's shoulder, not hiding the admiration in her voice. "They're looking pretty good out there. Who knew Ryan had it in him?"

Lila sighed. "Not bad."

Lacey blew the whistle around her neck, and a string of kids sat crisscross on the deck outside the restaurant. "Okay, Macaws! You ready to head back to practice for your show?" The kids cawed with excitement. This group was easier to manage than the littler kids. Lila wouldn't even have minded Twilight duty with this crowd, but she'd been seated with

Tustin at breakfast and he had ordered her to take the night off to experience her first *formal evening* from a guest's point of view. She thought that was odd, but he didn't have to twist her arm. That meant time with Jackson.

"Lacey?" she asked as they walked the kids past the pool, back to Little Delights. "What do you wear on formal night?"

"I have this little black number I wore the one time I was lucky enough to get off Twilight duty."

Lila nodded. She could wear her classic black dress, but it lacked luster. It was amazing how being in love could make a person want to go out and buy a whole new wardrobe. Not that her budget would allow it.

"What are you planning to wear?" Lacey asked her.

"Nothing exciting."

"After what happened with Jackson? He's got the night off. I heard him tell Ryan he planned to spend it with you."

"I know. But I don't have time to go out and buy anything. Even if I did, I can't afford it. I'm saving all my money for school."

"So you've mentioned a few thousand times. Hey, don't look so glum." Lacey's eyes lit up. "I bought this little white dress, very chic, at the beginning of the season, but I haven't had the chance to wear it yet. You can borrow it."

Lila's spirits lifted. Lacey had great style. "You wouldn't mind?"

"If it'll get you in with Jackson Koble, it's for a good cause."

Lila smiled. "I think I'm already in. But I'd love to make tonight special."

Lacey winked. "A man like that is bound to be hard to hold. The dress will help. I'll drop it off around seven."

Lila laughed, but underneath her nerves pricked. Yesterday, she'd felt so sure of herself. Now she was starting to feel inadequate. Jackson was perfect in so many ways, and she was . . . well, just Lila. Maybe Lacey's dress would help boost her confidence. She had no doubt that if it belonged to Lacey it'd be a showstopper.

"I wanted to borrow a dress, not a Band-Aid." Lila groaned when she saw the fabric clinging to the hanger. Lila's roommates were already dressed and downstairs.

"Quick, let me see it on," Lacey said. "I have ten minutes before I need to be back to work."

Lila eyed the dress, nothing more than an elongated tube top; it had a thin strap that tied behind the neck centered at the top. It would hug every curve. Lila felt grateful that working all day and most of the night kept her active. She'd been able to keep off the pounds despite the occasional lunch of mini-hamburgers that she downed at Little Delights. She took the hanger from Lacey and slipped behind the bathroom door, emerging a minute later. It didn't take long to secure a Band-Aid.

"Wowza," Lacey said. "I'll remind you to thank me later."

The pool area outside the main restaurant had transformed to a mystical fairyland. Tiny colored lanterns draped the trellises that arched over the entrance. Strings of sparkling white lights were wrapped around every tree trunk, and candles on lotus leaves floated in the pool. Jazz piano drifted through the outdoor speakers situated along the pathway. Even the humidity had cooperated and dropped for the night. The usually boisterous voices of the guests and staff were hushed and intimate.

Lila made her way to Sophie, who was at the hostess podium.

"Lila!" she squealed. "You're *stunning*. Jackson's going to eat you up!" Her eyes twinkled.

Boy, does news travel fast around here. But she didn't mind. This was news she wanted to shout from the rooftops. She still had trouble believing Jackson had chosen her.

"Think you can seat me at his table?"

Sophie laughed. "That's the plan."

Lila let her eyes drift over the room. She didn't see Jackson anywhere. Sophie led her past the elegant tables throughout the restaurant, past the buffet line, and toward the roped-off area near where Little Delights had eaten hours earlier.

"Um, where are we going?" Lila followed Sophie as she ducked under the ropes.

Sophie didn't answer. She led Lila through the double French doors facing the river. On the otherwise deserted patio, Jackson sat at a table for two. A vase holding a branch blooming with two white flowers, bright yellow at their centers, adorned the table. A bottle of champagne waited in an ice bucket. More paper lanterns swung from the rafters, and Lila could make out the lights of distant boats on the river. But it was Jackson who took Lila's breath away.

He stood to greet her, smoothing his black jacket in a nervous gesture. She could make out the hard lines of his body under the fine material, but he didn't look uncomfortable or stilted. He seemed made to wear Armani. Lila wondered if he'd borrowed the suit, the way she'd borrowed the dress. No way could he afford something so fine. She rejected the idea when she noticed how well it fit him. Lila swallowed the lump in her throat and turned to thank Sophie, but she'd already flitted inside. Lila turned back to Jackson, whose eyes looked too wide in his face as he took in her dress.

He cleared his throat, but it came out husky. "You look . . . enchanting."

Lila stepped forward to join him at the table. Her blood raced through her veins. "Thanks." She willed her voice not to shake. What was the matter with her? "So do you."

Jackson rounded the table to pull out her chair and then sat back in his own. "Champagne?" He lifted the bottle.

Lila read the label, shocked to see it was an expensive, well-known brand. She cringed. She didn't want him to feel like he had to break the bank just to impress her. She liked him for who he was. Maybe if they didn't open the bottle he could return it.

Jackson popped the cork and poured the amber fluid before she could protest.

Too late. Might as well enjoy it. Maybe it'll take the edge off my nerves.

"You didn't have to," she said.

"I wanted to. It's supposed to go well with the catch of the day."

"Well, then who am I to resist?" Lila smiled.

Jackson raised his glass in a toast and gave her a crooked smile. "To the catch of the day."

Lila swallowed the lump in her throat and clicked her glass against his. She took a long sip, letting the bubbles sail through her bloodstream, tingling from head to toe. "It's wonderful. Thanks."

"I hope you don't mind that I ordered for us."

"Ordered? Dinner is buffet style."

Jackson gave her another sly grin, and Lila's heart melted in her chest. She'd have to warn him not to do that unless he wanted to mop her up from the floor.

"Not for us tonight, it isn't. I talked Sophie into arranging something special with Emilio. He'll bring our first course in a minute."

Good old Sophie, Lila thought. The people around here might be beautiful, but most weren't shallow, as might be expected. She leaned in to smell the flowers on the table. "Mmm. What is this?"

"A Cherokee rose," Jackson explained. "It's the state flower of Georgia. I thought you might like it. I *wanted* to bring you the state flower of Arizona, to remind you of home, until I found out it was a saguaro cactus."

Lila laughed. "Good call. It's lovely, thank you. But, Jackson, you didn't have to go to all this expense. I'm happy just to be able to spend time with you."

Jackson reached across the table, taking her hands in his. He lifted her fingers to his lips and placed a tender kiss there.

The moment the warmth touched her skin, an electric current shot from her fingers straight to her heart. Jackson raised his eyes to hers, lids heavy; his lips lingered. He parted his mouth to say something, but Emilio appeared with two plates of prosciutto and melon.

Jackson released her hands, and Lila placed one over her heart to calm the hammering. Emilio smiled without speaking, then slipped away.

"Saved by the antipasta," Lila laughed, her voice sounding tinny and full of nerves.

Jackson's forehead crinkled. "Do you *need* saving?"

Lila stuck her fork into the melon and lifted it to her mouth. "I meant *you.*"

Jackson laughed. It mingled with the jazz and intensified the tingling in Lila's toes. She took another long draw from her champagne glass.

"Easy there. I want a dance before this night is through, and I don't want you unconscious for it. Am I making you nervous?"

"Exceedingly." Lila finished the liquid in her glass and held it out for more.

Jackson licked his lips and smiled. "Then I'd better take that dance now."

He rose, unbuttoned his jacket, and swung it over his shoulder. Then he pulled Lila's chair out for her. She stood, legs too wobbly for the amount of champagne she'd consumed. Jackson wrapped his jacket around her bare shoulders, then grasped her hand. Rather than heading for a clear spot on the deck, he kicked off his shoes, bent down to strip Lila's sandals from her feet, and led her to the beach.

As the speakers crooned, Jackson wrapped his free arm around Lila, drawing her close to him. She could feel the thrumming of his heartbeat through his tailored shirt. Strong and regular at first, it gathered intensity as he held her. She rested her head on his shoulder, letting her lips graze his neck.

He smelled just as she remembered, like the warm sun, the

salty breeze, and something sweet she couldn't place. Maybe it was the Cherokee rose. The sand felt cool between her toes. She let her eyes flutter shut as Jackson swayed to the music. By the time they reached the waterline, the music was a memory. Jackson released her body, but he kept her hand and they walked along the shore, leaving a trail of wet footprints in the sand. Lila looked up at him, the moonlight glowing in a halo around his head, and felt the strength of her own affection reflected in his eyes. She took in a deep breath of night air and shivered.

"You're cold?" Concern etched Jackson's voice.

"No." Lila was surprised by the hoarseness of her tone.

"Scared?"

"A little," Lila admitted.

"Me too." He took the jacket from her shoulders and laid it on a dry spot of beach. He helped her down, then sat beside her. Warmth emanated from his body. He reached over to tuck a strand of hair that had fallen over her eyes behind her ear. "This is new to me."

Lila looked at him with what she knew was obvious skepticism. He might not be the player she'd once thought him, but she knew he had had plenty of experience. She couldn't help it when the words came out sarcastic. "Making love is new to you?"

"*Being* in love," he whispered into her hair.

Being in love. Warmth surged through her as Jackson lowered his lips to hers. He wasn't going to push himself at her, even if she'd wanted him to. He was going after her heart. She just hoped he'd be careful with it. She was pretty sure it couldn't withstand the pain of losing him once she'd let him in.

She crushed against Jackson's chest, desperate to be close to him. Her eyes stung with emotion. His hands wrapped around her waist, stroking the small of her back through the dress.

"I could die happy right now," she whispered against his lips.

"I've never felt this way before, Lila."

Lila opened her mouth to respond, to tell him the same, but she didn't have the breath. Instead she focused on the exhilarating sensations whirling through her. She watched the trickle of colors light the back of her eyelids and fell deeper into the vacuum they'd created.

Jackson made an effort to pull away, and awareness drifted back to Lila. She'd been clutching his shoulders and pressing into him.

A look of wariness took over his face. When he spoke, his voice was hoarse. "I'm beginning to notice there's not much material to that dress." He looked almost apologetic.

Lila's own voice sounded small to her ears. "You're beginning to notice?"

"I'm afraid I'll stop noticing much of anything else if we carry on."

Lila propped herself on one elbow and raised an eyebrow. "You want to stop kissing me?"

Jackson wedged an arm under her and held her close. Lila could feel his heartbeat slowing to its regular pattern. "I'd like to kiss you until the tide goes out, but we should stop."

Lila looked at him in disbelief. She was relieved, but *still*.

Jackson gave her a tender kiss on the nose. "I want more of you than what's packed into this dress, Lila. I'm yours, *really* yours, for as long as you want me."

Lila wanted to hold on to that promise, that fantasy. He was so different from Brody, who'd always tried for more than she was willing to give. It's no wonder he'd cheated on her. But Jackson was telling her that he was hers for as long as she wanted, and it felt like she'd always want him. She tried not to think about going back to Scottsdale soon. Back to school and to reality. She had no doubt Jackson would stay on for another season or maybe transfer to another resort like some of the staff did. He clearly had a passion for the water, and no doubt he needed the money.

Her eyes filled with tears at the thought of having to give him up. She was glad it was too dark for him to see. She hadn't risked her heart with Brody, only her pride and money. But this time, everything was different.

Chapter Sixteen

BE A GENEROUS FRIEND AND A FAIR ENEMY;
OR IS THAT, ALL'S FAIR IN LOVE AND WAR?
LUCKY NUMBERS: 36 5 10 22 21 4

Lila rose at the crack of dawn to write in her journal. She couldn't resist capturing the cascade of emotions she'd experienced with Jackson. Thinking of it made color rush to her cheeks. Last night had been incredible. *He'd* been incredible. She sighed as she finished the page, earmarked it with the paper clip, then slipped the envelope of cash under the clip. Usually, she'd put the journal into her beach bag, to keep an eye on it now that it had started to have some real value, but today she'd be taking the Little Delights swimming, and she didn't want to risk leaving those juicy tidbits lying around for anyone to pick up. Not to mention her nest egg. Today she'd place her future under lock and key.

She stooped over the room safe, which was hidden behind Pascalle's slinky dresses. It blinked red. She punched in the numbers again and got the same response.

"Did you change the safe combination?" Lila asked Pascalle.

Pascalle spent more time in the room since Drew had picked up additional hours working Guy's vacated public relations position. That made a funny picture. Drew off the tennis courts, being civil to fellow staff members and guests.

Pascalle paused from running a brush through her tresses. "Not me. Maybe Regina?"

115

Lila peered at Regina's cot. She was still asleep. No way would Lila interrupt her. Regina was bristly enough with a full night's sleep.

"I'll ask her later." Lila searched for a place for her journal and its stash of cash among the shelves, but every inch was jam-packed. She settled on tucking it inside the spare pillow at the top of the closet. She could hardly reach it herself, so she figured no one else would bother.

"Good idea," Pascalle winked.

"Brody here," a groggy voice answered the phone.

"*Lila's* Brody?" Jenna asked, opting for a direct approach. From what she could gather, Brody and Lila had dated at one point, and now he wanted her back. As far as Jenna was concerned, this conversation was a win-win. Either she could talk him into coming after Lila to take her away from Jackson, or Jenna could use him to scare Lila away from the resort . . . and from Jackson. Either way, she needed Brody on-site for a while.

"You know Lila?" His voice perked up.

"Lila and I are good friends. She talks about you all the time, but she didn't have the nerve to call."

Brody grunted.

Jenna wondered if he was this slow all the time or if it was just the time difference and the early hour. "Lila is too proud to admit she made a mistake leaving you." Jenna held her breath. Assuming Lila had left Brody was a gamble.

"She realized her mistake, huh?"

Jenna let out the breath. "She did. But she's too proud to come crawling to you. If you still want her, you need to come down here and get her."

"To Florida? That would be expensive. I'm saving up for a ski trip—"

Jenna's patience snapped. "I work in reception for Encantadora. If you can manage to spring for the ticket, I can make your stay complimentary for a few days."

"Free? Food and everything?"

"Yes." Lila and this guy deserved each other.

"Drinks?"

"Included at meals."

"Huh." Silence filled the line while Brody apparently calculated his ability to scrape together cash for transportation. "Maybe Lila will pay me back for the plane ticket."

"Probably. For now, I think we should keep it a surprise."

"Lila never liked surprises."

Jenna wondered just what kind of surprises he'd sprung on Lila in the past, but decided she deserved them—the conceited way she'd weaseled her way into this job, acting like she owned the place and all the best-looking guys in it.

"I'm sure she'll like this one. When can I expect you? How about tomorrow?"

"I guess . . ."

"Perfect. Ask for Jenna when you arrive. I'll make sure you don't run into Lila before we're ready."

"Hey, Jenna's a hot name . . . maybe if it doesn't work out with Lila, you and I could—"

Jenna hung up on him. What had Lila seen in this guy? He must be *really* good looking to put up with that. She just hoped the guy could manage to woo Lila back.

Jenna rejoined Bertrand at the front counter just as Pascalle called to him on her way to visit Drew in his temporary office down the hall.

"Morning, Bertrand. Can you send someone up to look at our safe? The lock's broken. We're reduced to stuffing our loot in old pillowcases and under mattresses." She laughed.

"I'll get the new guy out within the hour. You don't need someone to be home, do you? I assume you don't have anything too valuable stashed away up there?"

"Given our salaries, that's a reasonable assumption."

Bertrand went to retrieve the maintenance form, and Jenna used the opportunity to peek at the mail cubbies. A postcard poking from Jackson's mail slot caught her eye. She plucked it out and scrutinized the picture. It was a scene of the old Las Vegas strip, with a neon cowboy waving his hat. She flipped it and read the feminine scrawl on the back twice before an addendum to her plan sprung to mind. "Well now, Jacky, you bad, bad boy . . . *what have we here?*"

Jackson knocked on Lila's door for the fourth time that morning, willing her to answer. He'd already been around to Little Delights, but she hadn't been there. Ryan told him she'd popped back to her room to change into a swimsuit to take the kids to the pool. They must have just missed each other. He looked over the courtyard, deciding what to do. He didn't want to leave without saying good-bye, and he hadn't gotten the chance last night to tell her he'd be gone for a few days. He smiled when he remembered what had occupied their time instead of small talk. After they'd found a slightly less private spot on the beach, so as not to tempt fate, they'd spent a lot more time lip-locked.

He glanced at his watch. Five minutes before his taxi was due. If he missed it, he wouldn't make his flight from Fort Lauderdale to Georgia. He really wanted to speak with Lila before he left—to let her know what was going on and to tell her when he'd be back. He also wouldn't mind a good-bye kiss. He sighed when he realized he wouldn't have time to track her down. He felt his pocket for the pencil and paper he'd used to jot down the cab company info. He'd have to settle for leaving a note. He ripped the paper in half and scrawled a message along the narrow strip. *Lila—I had to leave for a few days, but will be back soon. I'll explain it all later. Miss you already. Yours, Jackson.*

Somewhat satisfied, he tucked the paper in the door and heaved his overnight bag over his shoulder before making his way toward the waiting cab.

Jenna watched Jackson jog down the path away from Lila's building and smiled to herself. She couldn't believe her luck.

It'd been fate to find out he was leaving for a few days while she enacted her plan. The slip of paper Jackson had left drew her eye. She looked around to be sure no one would see, then ripped the paper after the first sentence so the note said simply: *I had to leave*. She read the half in her hand with disgust. *Smitten after one week. Poor deluded guy*. Jackson would thank her for this someday.

If Brody arrived tomorrow, she'd only need a day or two to set things in motion. A noise on the stairs jolted her. She ducked into the door well next door, lingering while the new maintenance man knocked at Lila's door, then slipped his master key into the lock and pushed the door open.

Jenna stepped up behind him. "Are you here to fix our safe?"

The man looked startled. "I got a work order here. I didn't think anyone would be home."

"It's about time. I just need to pop in to change for yoga before you go in."

The man mumbled something unintelligible, but he backed away so that Jenna could enter. She ducked in and closed the door in his face, then scanned the room. *If I were Lila, where would I squirrel away my money?* Pascalle had mentioned mattresses and pillowcases. Jenna shoved her arm underneath Lila's cot, then Regina's, Pascalle's, and Sophie's. Nothing. She undressed the pillows. Still no luck.

The maintenance man knocked twice. "Want me to come back later?"

"I'll be right out." She dropped what was left of Jackson's note on Lila's bed, then moved to the bathroom area. She spied the two extra pillows at the top of the closet. Stepping on a suitcase wedged into the corner so that she could stretch up and reach the corner of the pillow, she tugged and it spilled, along with its hidden contents, onto the floor.

Bingo.

* * *

"What are you doing here?" Jenna eyed Ryan with distaste when she saw him helping passengers onto Jackson's boat. "I thought the tours would be canceled with Jackson away."

"Not a chance. The river tour is one of the most popular attractions. Tustin's letting me fill in until Jackson gets back. You getting on or what?" Ryan asked.

"Obviously." She ignored his helping hand and shimmied up the ladder.

Ryan shrugged and turned a sunny smile to the next couple in line. "Welcome! Beautiful morning for a river tour!"

Jenna made her way to the back of the boat.

"Is that an alligator?" she shrieked, pointing downriver.

Dozens of heads swiveled. When she felt confident no one was paying attention to her, she shoved Lila's journal onto an upper shelf that was holding extra life vests. She placed it far enough back so it wouldn't be obvious, but close enough that if someone were looking, they'd find it. Now that it was out of her possession, the sooner the better. "My mistake; it's just a log." She smiled and weaved back to the front of the boat. Ryan was just taking up the anchor.

"I need to get off," she said.

"We're just about to leave," Ryan said.

"I think I'm going to throw up." Jenna cupped her hand over her mouth and made a retching sound.

"Whoa! Make way for the pretty lady, folks." Ryan handed her down with superspeed. "Maybe you'd better stick to land sports," he told her. "Not everyone is cut out for the sea."

"It's a river tour, you idiot."

"You have a great day too, miss." Ryan mock saluted her, then turned toward his guests.

Jenna gave him a patronizing smirk and made her way down the pier. Only one more wheel to set into motion.

Chapter Seventeen

Lila hummed as she made her way back to the room. Today had been a spectacular day. The sun had shone, and the river had sparkled blue and green. And the day was about to get better. She hadn't seen Jackson all day, but she knew he'd be at dinner because she'd heard through the grapevine that Ryan was running the boat tour that night. That must mean Jackson had finagled some time off, hopefully to spend with her.

She swiped her key card in the door and pushed it open. Dropping her pool towel on her cot, she stripped and headed for the shower. If she got ready quickly, she'd have time to write before dinner. She couldn't wait to get to her favorite spot on the deck to watch the sunset with her journal in front of her. Maybe Jackson would be there, reading his mail.

She was brushing her teeth when she heard someone enter the room.

"Big night tonight?" Regina called. Regina had been talkative, at least by her standards, since the Guy incident. Lila found she enjoyed it.

"Just trying to get to dinner early," Lila answered.

"I'm surprised you're in such a hurry, with Jackson gone."

"What do you mean?" A sinking feeling elbowed in on Lila's euphoria.

"He left a note—if you can call it that. I also heard it from Tustin."

Lila dried her face and rushed into the room. "Where?"

Regina jerked her chin toward the cot and a scrap of paper.

Lila stood over the bed, clenching the towel around her and staring at the meager note. *Where would he have gone? Why wouldn't he have said good-bye? And how had he gotten in the room?* Lila tried to suppress the foreboding that crept through her. At least he'd left her a message. That meant something. Maybe he was off-site to run a quick errand. She read the message again. There wasn't much to it. A terrible thought struck her. Maybe he had a family emergency or something. Lila felt her face drain of color. She closed her eyes and prayed she was wrong. He'd already alluded to losing enough people he'd cared about. She wished she could be there for him, wherever he was.

"Everything okay?" Regina asked.

"Sure. I just hope everything is okay with . . . his family and all. I'm assuming he had some sort of family emergency."

"I'm pretty sure his mom and dad were all the family he had."

"He's an only child?" Lila said, trying not to feel guilty about how little she knew about her new boyfriend. *So what if we haven't shared every detail of our lives yet? We hadn't had the chance to talk much about the past. Or maybe I've been intentionally avoiding it.* She'd been hoping to make up for lost time tonight. "He has nobody?" Lila said more to herself than to Regina.

"He's not forthcoming about his personal life. The guy likes his privacy. I know a little because I questioned why Tustin cut him so much slack. I used to think it's because he was down on his luck or something, but now I think it's because Jackson's so good at his job and Tustin likes him."

Lila thought about it. Jackson gave off a lot of vibes; most had either thrilled or terrified her from the beginning, but being down on his luck hadn't been one of them. She refused to believe that Jackson was here because he didn't have any other ambitions or options. Lila pulled the towel off her head. No use worrying about it now. She would throw herself into her work while he was gone, maybe write a few more fortunes for Joshua, and then ask Jackson all about it when he returned. Not *every* night could be a fairy tale.

She threw on her outfit and spent a minimal amount of time on her hair. The short, all-black dress she'd chosen to borrow from Pascalle no longer held the same appeal, but it had the benefit of distracting people from her hair and makeup, so she could let both of those slide a little. She reached for the pillow at the top of the closet. Her hand patted the top of the pillow, then flipped it over and patted the bottom. Something was wrong. She whipped the pillow off the shelf and searched it thoroughly; then she searched the top shelf and every inch of the closet floor. Her journal was missing.

Panic jerked through her. "Regina? Have you seen my journal?"

She looked up from polishing her toes. "That ratty notebook you're always carrying around? No. Need some help looking?"

"I've already looked everywhere. I can't find it." Lila's voice felt constricted in her throat.

Pascalle rushed through the door with a whoosh of humidity. She threw her yoga mat at the foot of her bed and smiled at Lila. "I hear you cracked our man of mystery. Why didn't you dish earlier?"

Lila froze. "What do you mean?"

Pascalle air-kissed her on both cheeks. "Dish. Give me the goods. Kiss and tell. What's the matter? You look pale."

"Lila lost her journal," Regina said.

Pascalle paused while unbraiding her hair. "Didn't you put it up on the shelf this morning?"

"No . . . yes. What do you mean by *our man of mystery?*"

Pascalle shrugged. "Nothing, just . . . you're the first person he's bothered to get close to. Even Traci couldn't get to him, and it's no secret he gets away with breaking most of the rules. It just creates an aura of mystery around him, that's all." She stepped past Lila and leaned on the middle shelf to peer up toward the top. "I don't see it."

"That's because it's *missing*," Regina said.

Lila's eyes drifted in and out of focus, one minute staring at Jackson's note, the next in the vague direction of Regina's toes. Regina must have noticed her conflicted expression because she came to Jackson's defense. "There's nothing mysterious about Jackson, Lila. He's just an ordinary guy—nothing to freak out about."

Just an ordinary guy, Lila thought. That was the problem. She'd had terrible luck with ordinary guys. They did ordinary things to her, like lying, and cheating, and stealing.

"Did you take the journal anywhere today?" Pascalle asked.

Lila shook her head. "No. We took the kids swimming, so I didn't bring it along."

"I wouldn't worry. It'll show up," she announced after scouring the closet a second time. She no doubt wondered why Lila would look so dejected over a lost journal. *But she has no idea what is written in there. Not to mention the three hundred dollars of hard-earned money for tuition.*

The sunset concert wasn't the same without her journal— or the possibility of running into Jackson. Lila watched some water-ski instructors enjoying themselves out on the river, a late-afternoon reprieve from their duties. She squinted into the buttery orange rays skipping off the wake, inhaled a deep breath, and let it out. It seemed unfair that Jackson would have to leave just when she'd been getting close to him. She hoped, for the hundredth time since finding his note, that he wouldn't be gone long.

Lost in thought, Lila didn't hear Jenna until she spoke. "I thought I'd find Jackson with you."

Lila looked up at her. She couldn't see Jenna's eyes because she had them shaded from the sun with one hand. The other held a stack of mail bound in a rubber band.

"He's not here," Lila said.

"So I gathered. He hasn't been by to pick up his mail in a while. His mail slot is spilling over. Where is he?"

Her words, always biting, felt painful tonight. Lila didn't want to admit she didn't know.

"Not here," Lila settled on responding.

Jenna clicked her tongue at her. "Trouble in paradise?"

"No, he just had to—"

"I don't care. Just give him his mail, okay?" She flipped the bundle on the chair next to Lila. A single postcard wafted to the deck beneath the chair.

"I can't take this. Jackson isn't—" Lila started to say that he wouldn't be back for a while, but Jenna had already stomped away.

Lila stared at the bundle, mostly fishing magazines and junk mail. She didn't want to intrude on his privacy, so she flipped the packet over so just the bottom magazine showed. She stooped over to pick up the postcard that had fallen loose. She didn't intend to read it, but the writing faced up, and the first sentence was written in a feminine scrawl that caught her eye. From there, she wouldn't have been able to stop reading had a hurricane swept in.

Jacky, thanks much for the flowers and candy. You're such the charmer. Having a great time. You'll be thrilled to know I got lucky for once and won some MONEY! I didn't even have to count cards like you said. By the way, you'll be happy to know I'm more in love than ever. And I miss you. Come back to me soon. XOXOX Emmalee. P.S. You were wrong about the KOA. It rocks.

Lila read the postcard two more times, flipping it over to study the picture of Las Vegas on the front. She felt caught in a crushing riptide pulling at her two beliefs: her trust in Jackson and the evidence on the card in front of her. *Could it be a trick of Jenna's?* No. The postmark was valid. Jenna wouldn't pull together such an elaborate scheme. Someone had sent this note to Jackson from Vegas. *Someone who still loved him and wanted him back.*

"Hey, Lila!" Ryan called from across the darkening beach. He was holding a girl's hand and waving something around in his free hand. Lila couldn't make it out against the blinding sunset.

"I'll give you a hint," Ryan called as he got closer. "It's a book."

Lila scrambled to shove the postcard in the center of the junk mail, then got to her feet as she watched Ryan approach.

"Is that what I think it is?" she called.

"If you think it's a sappy story about some chick falling in love against her better judgment, then yes."

Lila's heart stopped beating. "You *read* it?" She wanted to jump down from the deck and tear it from his grip, then shred the pages she'd written about Jackson into a million pieces and drown them in the river. But it wasn't Ryan's fault that Jackson had gotten a postcard from some girl named Emmalee. Some girl without scruples, if the card-counting remark was any indication.

"It was a lucky guess," Ryan said.

Lila's chest compressed. He hadn't read it. She forced a smile of gratitude. He'd never know her soul was crumbling inside. "Sorry, I—" Lila let her voice drop when Ryan and the girl reached the deck and she could see their faces. *Lacey.* Lila's eyes widened with the unspoken question.

Lacey shrugged. "He wore me down."

In spite of the turmoil inside Lila, she grinned at Ryan and Lacey. She couldn't help but be happy for her two closest friends at the resort. "I can't say I'm not surprised, but I *am* happy for you," she said. Lila took the journal from Ryan, hugging it to her, then hugging Ryan. "*Thank you.* Where'd you find it?"

"It fell off the storage shelf when I was docking the Navigator."

The smile slid off Lila's face. "You found my journal on the Navigator?"

Ryan nuzzled Lacey's ear and she swatted him away. "We figured you left it there when you went off with Jackson."

"We took the catamaran," Lila whispered.

Ryan squinted. "Huh. Weird."

Lacey eyed Lila. "You all right?"

Lila straightened, clutching the journal. "Sure. And I think you're right, Ryan. Jackson and I did stop off at the Navigator first. I forgot."

"Cool." Ryan nipped at Lacey's cheek.

Lacey gave up fighting him. "I've got to go, Don Juan. Twilight calls."

Ryan grinned. "Me too, but I need a shower first. I'll catch up with you later. See ya, Lila."

After they'd gone, Lila plopped into the deck chair, staring at Jackson's mail. After a long minute, she picked it up and dropped it in her bag. She'd return it to reception the first chance she got, and she'd hold off on making any judgments against Jackson until he got back and had the chance to explain. *If* he came back to explain. With that decision made, she felt a little better and turned to her journal. She opened it to the page she'd marked with the paper clip, and her world dropped out from under her.

The journal was marked on the same page she'd left it, but the envelope, and all the cash she'd been saving, was gone.

Chapter Eighteen

YOU WILL CREATE A UNIQUE OPPORTUNITY FOR YOURSELF;
DON'T JUST SIT THERE, TAKE IT!
LUCKY NUMBERS: 6 14 17 27 30 34

Jackson couldn't believe he'd been away from Tybee nearly four months already. As he pulled the rental car to a stop in front of Cast-a-Line Charters and Tours, he felt a surge of peace he hadn't experienced in a long while. Leaving the windows to the rental rolled down, Jackson opened the door and headed toward the familiar building. He could see Mrs. Meeny squatting like a toad behind the desk in a characteristic floral-print blouse. She hadn't noticed him yet, so instead of going inside, he veered toward the pier, where the skiff was tethered. Ordinarily, he would be surprised by this. Cast-a-Line was almost always booked back-to-back for skiff tours, but they still had a week before peak season hit, and he'd given Manny instructions to close down for a few days to prep for a quick trip to Mexico. Jackson planned to tackle Puerto Rico himself, as he'd only have to be away from Lila for a few days. If Manny thought Mexico looked good, Jackson would fly down there next month to confirm it. Maybe he'd be able to talk Lila into joining him by then.

Jackson stepped onto the boat and sunk into the cushion on the passenger bench. He stared over the water, where the sun was just beginning to set. His father had loved to go out in the skiff this time of day, when the wildlife in the marshes and inlets was really alive. Jackson toyed with the idea of going out for a spin, but he had only a few hours to spare before he had to be back at the airport for his flight. He wouldn't have stopped over in Georgia at all if he hadn't thought he needed to recapture the essence of the original Cast-a-Line before assessing whether the new property would be as successful.

His father had been big on essence. "Go ahead and make your charts and graphs, boy," he'd say. "We didn't educate you for nothing. But it's your gut that will tell you if the place has essence. Can't succeed without it."

Well, at least Dad got it right with this place. And I got it right with Lila. Now I just need to apply the principle to business. I won't let you down, Dad.

He rose to disembark and found a family of three working their way down the pier. A boy of about five wearing a SPRING BREAK T-shirt trailed behind his parents. He leaned over the water to watch the minnows.

"You taking her out?" a rotund man in a bright yellow shirt asked. "The lady inside said there'd be no more tours till the day after tomorrow, but I saw you and thought I'd ask."

"She's right. But we'll be back in full swing by Wednesday," Jackson affirmed.

The man's wife, a stout woman with a no-nonsense look about her, addressed her son. "Sorry, Robbie. No boat ride today."

The boy pouted. "Aw. I wanted to see the sea turtles."

"Stop whining. You can see them in the video room at the Marine Center back on the mainland."

Jackson looked at them agog. No way was he going to let this kid spend his vacation watching turtles on television when Jackson knew the perfect spot to view them in their natural habitat. It was a bit too early in the season to see them climb the beach to nest, but at least they wouldn't be digitally reformatted on a wide-screen.

"Robbie, is it? How'd you like to see some real flesh-and-blood reptiles?" Jackson asked.

The man eyed him. "You sure you can do that? The lady said you were closed."

"I can do whatever I want," Jackson said. "I'm the boss. It's about time I start acting like it."

Lila ran through the deserted golf course, not bothering to muffle her tears. She hadn't passed another soul for a good half mile anyway. At this hour, she wasn't likely to. Unless you counted the alligators. As far as Lila was concerned, the alligators would be a welcome relief from the pain she felt over what she'd learned today. There was no denying it. Some girl Jackson had sent flowers and candy to wanted him back. Even if his feelings had changed, he was gone without explanation, along with all of Lila's money. Her book had been found on *his* boat. He'd been in her room at some point, and he knew about both the journal and the envelope. The situation looked grim.

She rummaged for any logical explanation, but came up short. Her mind wanted to defend him, but it was easier to believe the handsome, talented Jackson had conned her, taken what he'd wanted, and left her holding the pieces. Lila stopped running and slowed to catch her breath. The combined effort of sobbing and running had exhausted her, as planned. The golf course was lit by a series of low-wattage lights, but it was still too dark to see clearly. She hoped she wouldn't really run across any alligators.

She thought back to the night that Jackson had followed her home from the Crab Shanty. Could he have feigned how much he cared for her? Lila stopped walking. She didn't think so. Wherever he was, whoever else loved him, Jackson had cared about her for a short time. She believed that much, didn't she?

Lila took in a breath of sprinkler-cooled air, then let it out. The pain of losing Jackson was unbearable. She wanted nothing more than to hide under the covers until morning, then call Cliff and beg for her old job back. But she knew she couldn't spend her whole life running away from liars like Brody, slimeballs like Guy, and utter heartbreakers like Jackson. The right thing to do was focus on her job until the next peak travel weeks passed, and then Cliff would probably hire her back in the office. She would call him first thing tomorrow to ask. In the meantime, she'd focus on her work and her friendships and keep men, *especially* Jackson, at bay.

Jackson stared out the window of the puddle jumper, his knees jammed against the seat in front of him. *What a complete waste of time this trip to Puerto Rico had been.* He couldn't believe Mr. Ramirez had almost taken him in. It was a good thing Jackson had forced the site visit, or he might have sunk a good portion of his father's hard-earned money into a black hole. The place Ramirez had wanted to sell him was a dump. The bay on the northeastern side of the island was impossible to reach by land because of a rocky limestone outcropping. One either had to traverse on foot over the eroding coast, or come by boat through the mangroves fringing the area or by sea. Still, Jackson had no doubt it'd been extraordinary once and still might be if it could be cleaned up and the erosion stopped.

Other than an amazing variety of birdlife peeking out from the mangroves, the only water wildlife Jackson had seen near the pier had been fighting for its life inside a plastic six-pack ring. Ramirez's so-called fleet of boats was unkempt and weatherbeaten. Jackson suspected the reason they didn't sink was the heavily buoyed rope tethering them to a dilapidated, hurricanedamaged pier.

In contrast, Jackson reflected on how stunning the island looked from the air. The mangroves fringing the shoreline and the occasional orange-red tops of flayboyan trees whispered *essence*. Jackson shook his head. He thought about the decision he'd made and wondered if he'd done the right thing. Would his father have done the same? The worst part about this little jaunt—or maybe the best, Jackson wasn't sure yet—was that he realized he missed the business. If he were honest with himself, he missed all aspects of it, paperwork and decisions included. He'd enjoyed the distraction of Encantadora, but maybe it was time to face the real world again.

He thought about Lila. Was she just a distraction too? She hadn't felt like one. She'd felt like a genuine and necessary part of his life, one he could picture fitting in with his real world. His heart rate escalated just thinking about her. Could he talk Lila into staying with him when he left Florida? Or would she be anxious to get home? As he stared out the window, his eyes focused on the dark blue horizon, and he thought about what he wanted to say to her.

He looked away long enough to punch Manny's number into his cell phone. After listening to Manny's monosyllabic report on the Rocky Point site, which translated to a glowing recommendation, Jackson ordered him straight home without making any promises to the seller. Jackson would discuss it later.

Jackson's flight landed in Fort Lauderdale in the late evening. After retrieving his duffel from the luggage carousel, Jackson picked his way through to the exit, where he planned to hail a cab. Road traffic swarmed the airport pickup zone despite the late hour. Jackson had to yell to inform the transportation coordinator of his destination.

"Hey—whoa!" a voice called from behind Jackson.

He turned to find a guy in his midtwenties, of average height, wearing reflective sunglasses. Since it was dark, Jackson wondered how the guy didn't trip over the curb.

"Hey, buddy, did you just say Encantadora resort?" the guy asked.

Jackson hesitated. He wasn't in the mood for chitchat. He just wanted to get back to see Lila. Besides, guys who called other guys *buddy,* when they didn't know them, had always irritated him.

The guy went on, even though Jackson hadn't answered. "I'm heading there too. Maybe we could share a ride? This trip is costing me a fortune as is."

Jackson sighed. "Yeah, sure. Whatever."

"Thanks a lot, buddy!" He smiled at the driver, showing teeth so white Jackson thought *he* should be the one wearing sunglasses.

Jackson moved to open the front door so he could sit shotgun, but a parrot had beaten him to it. Jackson raised an eyebrow at the driver, who apologized in a thick accent.

"I am sorry. It is only for tonight. My sister, she is taking the bird for me, but I have to wait until my shift is over to drop her off. The bird, she is no problem. She is clean, and she stay in her cage."

Tired and irritated, Jackson slipped into the backseat next to Sunglasses Guy and rubbed the bridge of his nose.

When it became clear to the driver that Jackson had no intention of objecting to his feathery companion, he became talkative again.

"The bird, she is good company for me. She can say a few words even. Do you want to hear?"

"No," Jackson said.

"Yes," Sunglasses Guy said.

"You will like it. Listen. Bebe, say *hello! hello!*"

The bird spouted off a phrase that sounded a lot like *whoo-whoo* and nothing like *hello*.

"I do not understand. Bebe always talks to me when I drive. Maybe she is nervous with her new friends."

Jackson tilted the tip of his Atlanta Braves ball cap low over his eyes and slouched in the seat, hoping to catch a few winks before reaching the resort. The cab driver and Sunglasses Guy had other plans. Bebe hadn't been in the mood to chat, but that didn't stop anyone else.

"Where do you come from, my friend?" the cabbie asked.

"Arizona," Sunglasses said.

"I have a cousin in Arizona. He works on the phone in a big office building. Do you work in big office building too?"

"Nah. I'm taking my time finishing school. I'm in no hurry.

Being a full-time student is living the good life—skiing just two hours away, swimming pools, and hot girls. It's sweet."

"But how do you earn the money if you are only a student?"

"Yeah, well, there's that. That's why it's important to hook up with a sensible chick. Someone fine to look at but who knows how to take care of a guy."

"There are women like that for the taking in Arizona?"

"Yeah, well, there used to be. Mine up and left for Florida. That's why I'm here—to let her come crawling back to me and to bring her home."

Jackson snorted, but he didn't venture any disparaging comments.

The driver sounded equally surprised. "I do not know many women who will crawl to a man. My sister, her husband he cheat on her, and she tell him to hit the road. She rather have Bebe than a good-for-nothing cheat."

"Easy now," Sunglasses objected.

"I did not mean you, sir. I am sure you are a fine gentleman. Your lady is, I am sure, lucky to have you come after her."

"Yeah, she is."

"Your lady, she is pretty?" the cabdriver asked.

"I wouldn't have her if she wasn't hot."

"Your lady is hot?"

"Darn straight Lila's hot. Best part is, she doesn't know it."

Jackson bolted up from his seat, and Sunglasses Guy threw himself against the door.

"Dude! Watch it," he said with accusing eyes.

Jackson glared at him through narrow slits. The sunglasses had slipped down the guy's nose, revealing weak blue eyes. A thousand thoughts and images flashed through Jackson's head . . . Sunglasses Guy catapulting out the cab window and landing facedown in the center freeway lane . . . Jackson's hand around Sunglasses Guy's throat, squeezing until his eyes bugged out. Then less satisfying images crept in, images that

made Jackson's stomach turn . . . Lila in the guy's scrawny
arms . . . Lila kissing him . . . Lila laughing with him . . .

Jackson clamped his teeth together. He knew he should talk
to Lila before doing anything impulsive. He told himself a
hundred times she wouldn't want him to break every one of
the guy's shiny teeth. She wouldn't want him to grab him by
the back of the head and press his face into the cab's sticky
vinyl for the rest of the trip.

"You scared the crap out of me, buddy!" Sunglasses Guy
whined. "Bad dream or something?"

With effort, Jackson willed his temper aside. "Nightmare."

"Uh-oh!" Bebe said, clear as a bell.

Chapter Nineteen

LUCK WILL BE YOURS WHEN YOU LEAST EXPECT IT;
UNFORTUNATELY, IT COMES IN TWO VARIETIES.
LUCKY NUMBERS: 6 14 20 11 2 34

Jenna watched both Jackson and the man she assumed was
Brody alight from the same cab. *This cannot be good.* She'd
have to act fast, or Brody might start spouting off about Lila,
and her plan would fall apart in the first two minutes.

"Jackson," she called. "Welcome back! Can you come here
a minute?" She shuffled through a stack of messages looking
for the one she needed.

"Not now, Jenna. I'm tired and in a bad mood."

"Sure, but you *really* need to see this message—it sounds
urgent."

Jackson made his way to reception. "What is it?"

Brody followed and stood elbow-to-elbow with Jackson at
the counter.

"Right here. It's from a girl named Emmalee. She says it's
important. You can use the phone behind reception if you want,"
Jenna offered, gesturing behind the desk.

"It's too late to call tonight." Jackson took the message and
turned to leave. He gave Brody an aggravated look over his
shoulder before starting toward his building. When he was out
of earshot, she turned back toward Brody.

"You're Brody?"

"Jenna?" He leaned in to view her name tag and let his eyes linger. "I expected a warmer welcome."

"You shared a taxi with *him?* He's your competition," Jenna hissed, indicating Jackson's retreating figure.

"What're you talking about? You said Lila was begging to have me back."

"That's not to say there aren't other guys who're interested. Did you get a good look at him? Jackson can be pretty persuasive."

Brody scowled. "Guy doesn't even like parrots."

Jenna ignored the weird comment. "We're going to have to be quick about this—and you're going to have to stick to the plan. You don't see Lila until I say so, got it?"

Brody eyed her with displeasure, but he nodded his agreement. "Whatever. Maybe I can squeeze in some vacation time. I noticed you have waterskiing. There's nothing I like more than to ski. My specialty is snow, but I'm pretty wicked on the water too."

Jenna's jaw clicked. "Waterskiing is *not* part of the plan. It's way too visible. You can stick to the land sports, but not until afternoon, when Lila won't be around. Come see me before you wander off to the restaurant too. I don't want you running into her by accident."

"Cripes, I have to ask your permission to eat? I'm not sure Lila's worth all this trouble."

"Did I mention there's some cash involved? At least three hundred dollars, maybe more."

Brody's eyes lit up.

"Think about it. Three hundred dollars to sit around a resort for a few days until your girlfriend comes running back to you. All you have to do is follow a few simple rules. It's a good deal."

"Maybe. But she better come *running,* or I'm going to start looking for a replacement."

*   *   *

"She's not here," Regina told Jackson through the crack in the door. She didn't look happy about being awakened at the late hour.

A cold feeling trickled down Jackson's spine. "No idea where she went?"

"I heard her tell Pascalle that she was going for a run."

Since when is Lila a runner? "It's pretty late for a run, don't you think?"

Regina shrugged.

"Is Pascalle here?"

"Pascalle is at the beach with Drew, and I wouldn't plan on interrupting them if I were you."

Jackson nodded his understanding. He needed to talk to Drew, too, but it could wait until morning. Lila couldn't. He let Regina go back to sleep and dragged a plastic chair onto the path outside the building to wait for Lila.

Not much later, footsteps awakened him from his light slumber. *Sunglasses Guy dragging his suitcase toward the building.*

"What are you, the keeper of this place?" Sunglasses Guy asked him.

Jackson stood so that he towered over the guy by several inches. "What did you say your name was?"

"Brody," he said, looking on edge.

"Well, Brody, I think you're lost. These accommodations are for staff members."

Brody produced his room key. "The girl at reception said it was being converted. I'm supposed to have Room 303."

Jackson looked at the key. "Jenna put you *here?* Why would she do that?" he said, more to himself than to Brody. She probably thought if she could get Brody and Lila back together, she'd have something to gain. *She had no idea how wrong she was.*

Jackson eyed Brody for a count before shrugging him off. Now was not the time or place. Besides, Lila wasn't even home yet. Better to have the guy tucked into bed than roaming the resort. Jackson intended to get to Lila first.

"Go ahead then, third floor. You'll have to hoof it."

Lila hadn't slept well. She stared in the mirror, willing her puffy eyes to recede. When she'd gotten back to her room last night she'd almost tripped over Jackson, who was asleep in a chair. She'd missed him so much it ached, but she'd forced herself to remember the postcard, the journal, the money, and his sudden departure. She didn't have the heart to hear excuses. Excuses were all she'd ever gotten from Brody. She knew that if she listened to Jackson she'd want to believe whatever he said, and she'd be crushed later to discover the white lies—or worse, that their whole relationship had been a hoax.

Someone knocked on the door. *Probably Jackson.* Lila scurried to the door and leaned with her back against it, chest heaving. Regina opened one eye and grunted. Pascalle and Sophie had left already for yoga, so no one else was home. The knocking intensified.

"Are you going to answer that, or do I have to lop his hand off at the wrist?" Regina asked.

"I can't," Lila mouthed, humiliated.

Regina rolled her eyes. "What is it now?"

Lila just shook her head. Jackson's voice came through the door.

"Look, Regina, I'm sorry to wake you, but I have to know if Lila's in there. I have to know if she made it home safe last night."

Regina eyed Lila clinging to the back of the door.

"Come on, Regina. You're killing me here. I *need* to know."

Lila nodded at Regina.

Regina yelled out from her bed. "Yeah, she made it home. Now bugger off so people around here can sleep."

Lila breathed relief. Somehow Regina had managed to spare Jackson's feelings, this time at least. For all he knew, she was too tired to answer the door. But she knew she couldn't expect Regina to cover for her forever. "Thanks," Lila mouthed, and she slumped to the floor against the door. Now she just had a call to make to get her life back on track.

The grounds were deserted except for a few early risers. No one bothered Lila in the restaurant, and she was relieved when she didn't run into Jackson. He was probably wiped out from his trip. *And from sitting up in a stiff plastic chair half the night.*

Lila grabbed a yogurt and a banana and headed toward Little Delights.

"You're here bright and early." Jules looked up from writing the daily schedule on the whiteboard.

"I couldn't sleep."

Jules eyed her with speculation. "Want some work to occupy your mind?"

Lila nodded, her throat tight. *Why was everyone so nice to her just when she was planning to leave?*

"Finish this up. A few early birds will make a drop-off just before the seven o'clock tennis lesson. You can help me watch them until the rest arrive."

Lila finished the whiteboard, then played dominos and checkers with the first girl dropped off. Ryan and Lacey joined her before long, and soon Little Delights bustled with activity. Lila threw herself into her work. The distraction numbed the pain a little but didn't extinguish it.

At eleven, Lila decided it was late enough in Scottsdale to call Cliff at the office. She stepped into the quietest corner she could find—a feat in Little Delights—and flipped open her cell phone. She knew it was against policy, but she was desperate. She dialed the number she'd memorized three months ago.

The receptionist answered on the first ring and sent her call straight through to Cliff.

"Lila?" Cliff said. "Tustin tells me you're doing a fantastic job. It sounds like you're making me proud."

Lila blenched. "Thanks."

"Just calling to touch base?" he asked.

"Not exactly. My . . . circumstances have changed a bit, and I was hoping you'd be able to take me back before the end of the season."

The line was silent for a few moments.

"You want to come back early?"

"If it's an option." Lila held her breath and crossed her fingers.

"Homesick?"

"Something like that."

"You're being vague, Lila. I know the job stretches your comfort zone, but Tustin said . . ."

"It's more than that. I just . . . I can't stay here much longer. Please don't ask me why," Lila said.

"I won't lie to you, Lila. We're not through the season yet, and business still isn't great. We're running pretty lean. Still, you've been a big help to Tustin, and if you can hold out another two weeks through spring break, I'd be willing to take you back on. I want to be clear. I'm not offering long-term guarantees. If things don't pick up in the next month or so, you could find yourself out of a job again."

"I'm willing to take my chances." Lila felt a boost in her spirits for the first time in three days.

"There's no training going on right now, so you'll have to help out with other things. We're interviewing for the on-locale staff positions, if you're willing to do that. Guess I'll have to add at least one more to the list for Little Delights in addition to the backfills for those who leave after spring break. It's not uncommon to get a few deserters this time of year."

Lila hoped he didn't think of her as a deserter. She would work twice as hard for him to prove her worth. "I'm sure what I've learned here will help me interview people. I know just what to look for."

"I'm counting on it. I'll talk to Tustin this week and arrange an exit date. You'll have to go to PR to book airline tickets home. Better book them now, before the fares spike."

Lila hung up just as someone tugged on the hem of her T-shirt. It was the girl she'd played checkers with during early drop-off that morning.

"Miss Lila, my eyes are all sticky," she said.

Lila crouched down for a better look.

Oh, no. Pink eye.

"Are you sure?" she asked the nurse for the third time.

"I'm sure, Lila. Pink eye is highly contagious. You can't go back to work or expose anyone else until you've been on the antibiotic for at least forty-eight hours. You can either go back to your room and lock down, or you can sleep in the infirmary for the next few days."

"I think I'll go to my room. My roommates have been sparse lately anyway, except for Regina."

"I think she can make alternative arrangements," the nurse said, looking toward Tustin's closed door. "The sooner we get this taken care of the better. Next week's going to be a mad-house. It's almost lucky you got it this week."

Right. *Lucky*. At least it was the perfect excuse for avoiding Jackson.

Jackson tried to distance himself from Jenna as far as the old phone cord would allow. He turned his back and waited until a woman's voice answered the line.

"Jacky?" Pug came on the line with her usual enthusiasm.

Jackson grinned. It felt great to hear her voice. "Hey, Pug. How was the honeymoon?"

"Heavenly. Didn't you get my postcard?"

"I don't remember seeing it." Jackson narrowed his eyes over his shoulder at Jenna.

"Probably Fish forgot to put a stamp on it or something. I *did* keep him distracted." She giggled.

"And that's my cue to change the subject. I'm glad you had a good time, and I'm even happier you're back."

"I wish I could say the same to you. When are you coming home, Jacky?"

"Not for some time. That's why I'm calling." Jenna edged into his peripheral view, miming something. He turned away.

"Dang it, Jackson. You've got to think of other people once in a while. I understood when you had to go off after . . . well, back then. But it's been a long time. You need to start worrying about your own customers. We're doing all right, but you're the one with the magic."

Jackson smiled again. He decided to stop her before she worked herself into a frenzy. "I'm not coming back to Tybee just yet, but I am coming back to the business. I'm planning to leave at the end of the month to set up the new shop."

The line went dead silent for a minute; then a high-pitched squeal burst from the receiver. Jackson had to hold the earpiece away until it stopped. It didn't end for a good while. Jenna even stopped miming to gape at him with burning curiosity. Probably most staff members didn't talk to crazy people in broad daylight.

"Listen up, Pug. I need some information."

"You bet, Jacky. What d'ya need?"

"I assume Manny's back from Mexico?"

"Yes sirree. Got back two days ago. Said the place was paradise on earth. Those are my words. Manny just said it was a go and showed me a bunch of photos he took."

"Where does it sit?"

"On a fine stretch of wide-open beach."

"Good, that's just what I was hoping to hear. It makes my decision all that much easier."

"You need me to e-mail you the photos before you buy the place?"

"Nope. I'm not planning to buy the place in Mexico."

Pug sounded taken aback. "Really? The Puerto Rico location must've been a peach."

"Exactly the opposite." Jackson remembered the rocky beach and the dilapidated pier.

"You find something in Florida you're going to buy?"

"Nope."

Pug sounded confused. "Okay, Jacky. I give up. Where are you setting up shop?"

"I'm having an offer drawn up for the Puerto Rico place." He thought about the wildlife he'd seen teeming at the edge of the mangroves. He had to believe it would flourish if he could get the immediate area cleaned up. He'd have to knock out and rebuild the pier too. It wouldn't be a small feat, but with a few new boats for deep sea fishing, a fleet of kayaks for the mangrove tours, and a little skiff for families with kids too young to kayak, he knew he could make a go of it.

Mr. Ramirez hadn't been at all put off by the preliminary offer Jackson had made, even though it was much lower than his asking price. Ramirez may have hoped to pass off the place sight unseen at a greater profit, but he recognized an opportunity when it was in front of him. Besides, Jackson had pretty much threatened to reveal him as a fraudster if he tried to hook someone else with his lies. It was amazing what a few blog entries could accomplish these days.

"I thought you said it wasn't nice."

"It's not," said Jackson. "But it has essence."

"Essence? That's it?"

"Never underestimate essence, Pug. Besides, it needs me more."

The line went quiet again. This time when Pug spoke her voice cracked a little. "Your pa would be proud, Jacky. You need us to come down and help set up the new shop?"

"I couldn't afford it. I need you to hold down the fort in Tybee and make sure I don't go bankrupt so that I can pour the money I need to into the new spot. Plus, I need you to keep an eye on Manny and Mrs. Meeny."

"Who're you going to get to help you?"

Jackson paused. "I've got a few ideas up my sleeve. It's just a matter of some careful negotiation so I don't leave Tustin in the lurch."

"I'm just so glad you're coming back where you belong. I was so worried about you."

"Nothing to worry about, Pug. For once in my life, it seems like I'm getting everything I ever wanted."

"I don't think I've ever heard you quite so optimistic, Jackson Koble. Wait a minute . . . could it be . . . ?"

"I've got to go, Pug. Someone's trying to get a message to me."

"Oh, no, you don't. I can read you like a book. I didn't believe I'd ever see the day. Jackson Koble, in *love?* Tell me she's not from Indiana."

"Arizona."

"Arizona! How does a boy born and bred in water fall for a landlocked desert girl?"

"Go ahead, make fun."

"Unlike *some* people, I have more sense than to poke fun at someone in love. I do want to meet her, though. To make sure she's good enough for you. You better not come home without her."

"I don't intend to."

When he'd hung up and turned back toward reception, Jenna looked a little put out. "I was trying to do you a favor, Jackson. To tell you about Lila."

"What about Lila?"

"She's got pink eye, and she can't have any visitors."

"Pink eye?" That was bad timing, but at least it was nothing serious. It also explained why he hadn't seen her.

Jenna nodded and handed him a stack of mail. Ryan walked up, looking surly.

"Hey, Ryan. You ready for those barefoot lessons?" Jackson asked.

Ryan threw back his head and groaned. "I can't believe it. I finally have two consecutive hours off in a row with an offer to learn the backward barefoot move, and Jenna sends for me to take Lila's place because of some conjunctions."

"Conjunctivitis, idiot," Jenna corrected him, and she went off to sort mail.

"Whatever. It's not fair."

Jackson laughed and patted him on the back. "Next time. In fact, I need to talk to you later on. Are you going to be at the bar tonight with Lacey?"

"Probably not. She's working Twilight. Why?"

"I'll fill you in as soon as I can, but let's just say I have a little opportunity I want to let you in on if you're interested."

Ryan winced. "Sounds like a bad investment scheme."

"I've got the money piece covered. What I'm looking for is some talent."

Ryan beamed. "Ah, well. If it's talent you're looking for, look no further."

Jackson clamped him on the shoulder, then made to leave. "We'll talk later. It's been a few days since I've been on the Navigator, and I'm sure it could use some cleaning up."

"I kept it in pretty good shape," Ryan protested. "I even made sure people didn't leave their junk behind—which is more than I can say for you."

"What do you mean?"

"You let Lila leave her notebook crammed up on one of the shelves. She freaked when she'd thought she lost it. I came off a hero finding it for her."

"Lila's notebook?"

"Yeah, but I'm just giving you a hard time, man. It's cool. You guys were probably a little . . . uh . . . distracted that night before you left."

"How did you—"

"No secrets in this place, man. The news was all over by breakfast. You're a hot commodity. Tears were shed, apparently."

"We didn't take the Navigator; we took a catamaran," Jackson said flatly. No wonder Lila was avoiding him. She was probably mortified by the whispers flying around half the resort and maybe worried what he'd think about them, given his reputation for relishing privacy. He'd have to make sure she knew he didn't care if the whole world knew they were in love. The more land sharks who knew about it, the better.

"Yeah, but Lila said you stopped at the Navigator first," Ryan said.

"No, we didn't."

Ryan scratched his head. "Huh."

"Did Lila take another tour while I was gone?"

"None of the staff took tours while you were gone—you'd think they were paranoid about my boating skills or something. Except Jenna, of all people. Good thing the guests didn't think the same, or Tustin would never let me out of diaper duty again."

"Jenna?"

"Jenna came onboard one afternoon, but she changed her mind. Seasickness."

"She got on and off the Navigator before you left dock?"

"Yeah. Why?"

Jackson stared at the back of Jenna's head as she tossed mail into the slots.

"Maybe nothing. Just trying to connect some dots."

"Lila, I don't care if you have tuberculosis. I'll take my chances," Jackson pleaded through the closed door. "I understand the quarantine, but you don't have to shut me out. I want to explain why I had to leave and talk about some ideas I have for the future."

The future, Lila thought. *What kind of future lives in half truths and suspicions?* Even if she could get past the journal and the money, what about Emmalee? She has a future in mind that includes Jackson too.

"Say something, Lila." Jackson leaned up against the door. He sounded as weary as she felt. "Open the door and let me talk to you . . . let me *see* you."

Lila pressed her lips shut so she wouldn't let something slip from her heart rather than from her good sense. He promised to be back after the evening's river tour, and his footsteps receded. Lila cried herself to sleep, not caring that it wasn't good for her eyes.

"Lila, honey? Are you all right?"

Lila shot up in the dark and stared at Pascalle through puffy lids.

"You're not supposed to be in here!" Lila's voice croaked.

"Relax, I'm just packing some things, but while I'm here, I have something to say."

Oh, no. Not Pascalle too.

"I don't know what's going on between you and Jackson, but the man is beside himself. He's crushed you won't speak to him. I've never seen him like this before. Lila?"

"I hear you."

"You *do* know I'm here for you if there's something you want to talk about, right? You can trust me to keep it just between the two of us."

"Uh-huh."

Pascalle sighed. "All right, but don't forget the offer, and try to show the man some mercy. He's smitten."

So he says, Lila thought. He sure had them all fooled, maybe even himself. Who juggled more than one woman and stole from the person he loves? Someone who's not in love, that's who. Someone like Brody. Tears stung her eyes again, but Lila couldn't bring herself to hate Jackson. All she felt was love and pain. Cry-yourself-to-sleep sort of pain.

Jenna knocked at ten the next morning. "Are you in there, Lila?"

"Where else would I be? I'm not allowed to come out for another day," Lila called from under the pillow.

"I just need to deliver a message."

"Slide it under the door." She didn't care if she was being rude. She was sick, crushed, and Jenna had never gone out of her way to be nice to her.

"It won't fit."

Lila stumbled from bed, flipped the door lock to the open position, and then ducked back under the covers. She heard Jenna open the door and shove something inside. When Lila looked up, she was bewildered to see that the package was Brody.

"You look like crap," Brody said, squinting.

Lila whipped the covers over her head to make the image of Brody go away. *This has to be a nightmare. He can't be here in my room.*

"They told me you were sick or something, but I thought you'd at least try to clean up a little for me."

Lila lowered the sheet. *Nope, he was still there.* "What are you doing here?" she said with such bitterness he flinched.

"Ah, that explains it. You didn't know I was coming today. I'll wait if you want to shower or something," Brody said. When Lila didn't move, he added, "What's wrong with you, anyway?"

Lila watched him make his way to the knickknacks, perfume bottles, and hairspray cans lining the long dresser in the room, fingering them as if he was already bored.

"Pink eye," Lila said.

Brody dropped his hands to his sides. "Nasty stuff. No offense, but keep your distance."

"I plan to," Lila said through gritted teeth.

"I've got ski plans for spring break. The last thing I need is impaired vision."

The mention of skiing was a mistake. Showing up in Florida was a mistake. *Being Brody* was a mistake. Lila felt the reeling shock vanish, replaced by rage.

"You slimy little weasel!" she yelled, her voice escalating with every syllable. "Get your despicable self out of my room before I have you thrown out!" She didn't wait for his response. She jumped from bed and shoved him with all her might toward the door. He backed into the hallway, and Lila slammed the door in his face. "And you owe me three thousand dollars!" she yelled at the closed door.

Pascalle burst through the door a moment later. "Pink eye or no pink eye, I heard you screaming from the courtyard. Now you're going to tell me what's going on. And I want the full story."

Chapter Twenty

Pascalle brought her drink from the bar to the group, dressed in all black and white, that was huddled around a poolside table. "Okay, people. Let's go over the facts again. Jackson and Lila finally hook up, then Jackson leaves. Lila's journal is lost, then found on Jackson's boat without the money. Jenna brings Jackson's mail, including a potentially incriminating postcard from someone named Emmalee, to Lila. Then Lila's leech of an ex-boyfriend shows up, acting like she should be grateful."

"Jackson's guilty," Traci said.

"No way," Ryan said. "The dude's whipped. He's not going to hurt Lila on purpose."

Lacey smiled and pinched him in the side. "He's got a point. Jackson is crushed by Lila's shutout."

Traci shook her head. "That doesn't mean he couldn't already belong to someone else back home. He wouldn't come near me. You have to admit, it's unusual."

Regina harrumphed. "Maybe he prefers brunets."

"Even if he has someone back home, it doesn't mean his feelings for Lila aren't real. People change. The man's not married," Pascalle pointed out.

"Not that we know of," Regina said.

151

"You don't have anyone back home, do you?" Lacey asked Ryan.

"Nope. I'm all yours, babe." He nuzzled her neck.

"Can we focus, please?" Pascalle rolled her eyes. "Here's another fact: Jackson's been meeting with Drew for legal advice. He won't give me details."

"Maybe Jackson's trying to get a quickie divorce," Ryan said.

"Drew's a property lawyer," Pascalle said. "I think we're going to have to make some basic assumptions here if we want to figure this out and help Lila."

Lacey nodded. "Let's assume he isn't married but maybe has a girl on the side. What would make him steal Lila's journal?"

"To get rid of evidence," Ryan said, as if they were all missing an obvious point. "Lila said she wrote about him. If he has a chick back home, he won't want that floating around."

"Then why didn't he dump the journal in the river?" Regina asked.

"Jackson dump something nonbiodegradable in the river? Are you crazy?" Ryan said.

"I think we can assume that Jackson doesn't plan to dump Lila and bury the evidence. He thinks he's in love with her. What else do you people have?" Pascalle drummed her fingers on the table.

"Money makes people do strange things," Lacey pointed out.

"You think Jackson would risk Lila for *three hundred dollars?*" Traci asked.

"How do you know how much money she had?" Lacey asked.

"I overheard her asking Bertrand where she could cash the check. She mentioned the amount."

"Jenna works with Bertrand," Pacalle pointed out. "And she's the one who gave Lila the postcard. She has access to all sorts of information, including anyone who calls or writes to the staff. As in *Brody.*"

"Jenna was on the boat before I found Lila's journal," Ryan added.

The little group leaned forward in their chairs, huddling closer.

"I think we're on to something." Lacey rubbed her palms together. "Jenna's an opportunist. I bet she saw a string of possibilities and tried to exploit each one, hoping to drive a wedge between Jackson and Lila."

"I think the money theory is more likely," Traci said.

"I don't," Regina said. "Tustin told me the reason Jackson left this week was to look at property in Puerto Rico. He's got his own business back home that's making money hand over fist. Tustin didn't think Jackson would stay on too much longer."

"Jackson's loaded?" Traci's eyes lit up like fireflies.

Pascalle took a sip of her drink. "That would explain why he's been talking to Drew. Maybe they're discussing property law. But where does Brody fit in?"

"He's been calling Lila nonstop since she got here," Lacey said. "Jenna probably thought he could talk Lila into getting back together."

"I doubt he has a chance," Pascalle said. "But to make sure of it, I think we should stage a little something to confuse him. I've seen the guy. It won't take much. Nothing a few of us girls, plus Isabelle and Henri, couldn't pull off."

Jenna glowered at Brody over the reception desk. She would not let him ruin her plans. "You're supposed to make her fall back in love."

"She's all ratty—it's not easy to snuggle up to someone crawling with germs. She scared me."

Jenna closed her eyes and took a breath. "I'll give you one chance to fix this, or you're out of here. Lila will be out of quarantine tomorrow. You're going to be the perfect gentleman and follow her every move until you convince her to get back with you."

Brody winced. "She'll see through that."

"Then let me call you a cab." Jenna picked up the phone.

"You'd do that to me?"

Jenna punched the numbers.

"Wait." Brody held up his hands in surrender. "I can do this. Tomorrow she'll be all cleaned up, and I can lay on the charm. You can count on me."

Jenna dropped the receiver. "I'll try to find a way to keep Jackson occupied in the meantime."

Traci strolled by the desk.

Jenna leaned in toward Brody. "Traci will be up for this. She's got a thing for Jackson, though he doesn't return it."

"The man's certifiably insane," Brody said, drooling at Traci in her colorful wrap.

"Traci, I think Jackson was looking for you earlier."

Traci raised one manicured eyebrow at Jenna. "I think you mean for Lila."

Brody's face flickered from fascination to irritation. "Lila's mine," he said.

Traci stepped closer, lingering near his shoulder. "Well, isn't that too bad? You're sort of cute."

The irritation vanished. Jenna raised both eyebrows at Traci and took another look at Brody.

Jenna continued, "Jackson is definitely looking for *you*, Traci. I think he's down at the beach. With his shirt off."

Traci didn't take her eyes from Brody. "Good for him."

"Hello there," someone called from behind the trio. Pascalle stopped in front of Brody. "I haven't seen you around. I'd have noticed."

Jenna's mouth dropped open. Sure, Brody was good looking, but he was nothing compared to the likes of Jackson or Drew.

"Back off, Pascalle," Traci said. "You have Drew."

Brody looked like he might burst at any moment. He did have broad shoulders.

"Hey, girls . . ." Lacey strolled up to reception. ". . . and *boy*." She stared at Brody.

"Need something, Lacey?" Jenna wasn't happy with the

macabre twist taking place. If Lila would respond to Brody like this, they'd be getting someplace, but these three were just plain annoying. *Since when did they take an interest in male guests, anyway?*

"Just picking up Ryan's mail," Lacey explained. "The man has me on errands every free second of my day. But *you . . .*" She turned back to Brody. "*You* look like you could take care of a girl."

Brody sputtered. Jenna thought that if an intelligent response was beyond him in the best of circumstances, it was just plain impossible with three women crowding him.

"Don't you people have work to do?" Jenna asked, including Brody in her scowl.

"Stick to the kiddies, Lacey," Pascalle said, ignoring Jenna and cooing in Brody's ear. "You like a woman who's flexible?"

"I—uh, well . . . I . . ." Brody's voice sounded dry.

Jenna prepared a scathing remark to send everyone scattering, but Isabelle rounded the corner. "Have you seen Henri?" she asked. "He's supposed to meet me here. If he's late again, he's finished." Her gaze fluttered around the reception area. "What is this?"

"Nothing," Jenna said. If Isabelle took an interest in Brody, he'd be toast.

"This doesn't look like nothing. It looks like girls fighting over something." Isabelle eyed Brody from a distance, then moved in closer.

Jenna flinched when Lacey stepped forward to block Isabelle's path. The one thing Isabelle's vanity couldn't resist was a challenge over a man.

"Mine," Pascalle eyed Isabelle with determination.

Isabelle's eyes narrowed and her interest in Brody piqued.

"I saw him first," Traci said.

Jenna threw her arms in the air. "Have you all lost your minds?"

Isabelle locked in on Brody. He was a man hypnotized. "What

makes you so special, hmm? Let me see." She inched past Lacey and placed her hand on the side of his face.

"Isabelle?" Henri's voice boomed through the lobby. "What are you doing with your hands on that boy?"

Jenna thought the term fitting. Henri's presence reduced other guys, Tustin and Jackson excepting, to mere adolescents.

Isabelle snapped her hand away from Brody. "I see nothing. I want nothing from him."

"Hey . . . ," Brody protested.

"Explain what you are doing with my Isabelle." Henri glared at him.

"I never touched her."

"I told you it was nothing," Isabelle said. "If you don't believe me, *we* are nothing." She cursed at Henri in Italian, then stormed away.

Henri's eyes never left Brody. "Are you saying that *goddess* came on to you?"

"They all did. Everyone saw." He looked from Pascalle to Lacey to Traci, whose expressions now only showed detached interest.

"It was my mistake. Nothing special here," Traci said.

What's going on? Jenna wondered. *Was it just that they were comparing Brody to Henri and regaining their sanity?*

Henri fumed. "You've insulted me. I want you out of here."

Brody assessed Henri and acquiesced. "Okay, sure."

"I mean leave the resort," Henri clarified.

"You can't kick me out. I'm a paying guest . . . sort of." Brody threw a pleading look at Jenna.

"What kind of a man turns to a woman to save him? I challenge you."

Brody paled. "To a fight?"

"A competition. If I win, you leave. If I lose, you can stay and have your choice of the ladies here—if any still want you."

Brody grinned at Pascalle and Lacey, confident in his own appeal. "What kind of competition?"

"A tennis match."

"No way. You look like a pro, and I don't play. What about skiing?"

"If you haven't noticed, we have no snow."

"Waterskiing, I meant."

Henri hesitated, looking from Pascalle to Lacey. Both appeared somewhat panicked.

"I don't water-ski," Henri said. "Tennis or nothing."

"Then nothing," Brody said, smug.

"*I'll* take that challenge." Jackson's voice cut across the room. "And I'll make it double or nothing."

Jenna's nerves flared in panic. How long had he been listening? Brody sized up Jackson and didn't see the threat. *The man must be blind or really stupid.*

"If you're the water-ski instructor, that wouldn't be fair," Brody said.

Jackson shook his head. "Why does everyone keep saying that?"

Brody eyed Jackson. "What's the double or nothing?"

"I hear there may be a job opening up here soon. If you lose, you're going to fill it."

Henri, Pascalle, and Lacey all looked at Jackson with shocked expressions.

Henri spoke. "You want him to *stay?*"

"If he wins, he stays and he gets the girl . . . if she wants him. If he loses, I get the girl, and he gets a new job."

"You're interested in that Isabelle chick too?" Brody asked.

Jackson gritted his teeth. "I'm talking about *Lila.*"

"Jackson is doing *what?*" Lila asked Pascalle and Lacey at breakfast the next day. A bite of omelet rested on a fork partway between her plate and mouth.

"He's challenging Brody to a water-ski competition. Winner takes all," Pascalle explained.

Lacey poured herself some more coffee.

Regina sat next to her, sipping tea from a paper to-go cup.

"Meaning exactly what?" Lila asked.

"*You,* I guess," Lacey said. "It's kind of flattering, don't you think?"

"Flattering? Did anyone stop to think what I might have to say in the matter?"

"What do you have to say?" Regina asked. "You think Jackson screwed you over?"

Lila dropped her fork, her appetite gone. "I don't know what to think."

"See, that's your problem," Regina explained. "You either trust the guy, or you don't. You need to make a decision and move on."

"I have," Lila whispered.

"Doesn't sound like it."

"Maybe I haven't got Jackson figured out, but I've decided I'm getting out of here as soon as I can, and in the meantime, I plan to avoid people who think they can trade me like they're Neanderthals."

Lacey, Pascalle, and Regina all exchanged glances.

"You're looking at this all wrong," Lacey said. "This is just Jackson's way of keeping you safe. He likes you . . . probably loves you."

"Yeah, well he probably throws the word around a lot. Looks like he's got women stashed all over the globe." Lila let her head drop into her hands. "I don't even know who he is. He goes running off to God knows where, sends romantic gifts to some mysterious woman who clearly needs money and who wants him to be with her . . . and . . ." She stopped herself before she could accuse him of stealing her journal and her cash. No need to completely drag the guy's reputation through the mud. She wasn't sure it was true anyway, despite the circumstantial evidence.

"You don't know if any of that is true," Pascalle argued.

"Yes, I do. He did leave without any explanation, he did

send a woman candy and flowers, and she did beg him to come back to her. Those are all facts."

"There could be a reasonable explanation," Lacey said.

"I'm sure he could think of one, but I'm not up for hearing it. I've been down this road too many times, and my last nightmare is still following me, if you haven't noticed."

"You can't compare Brody to Jackson. Brody's a schmuck, Jackson's the good guy," Regina said.

They stared at each other a moment. "Maybe, but it's obvious someone already has a claim on him. I'm doing them a favor by bowing out."

Pascalle took a spoonful of yogurt. "I doubt he'll see it that way."

"You'll still watch the competition, right?" Lacey asked.

Lila shook her head. "I'm tired of playacting. I'm going back to the real world." She pushed back from the table. "You're great friends, and I appreciate what you're trying to do. But I've got only two more weeks here, and then I'm going back to my old job." She held back a tear. "I plan to hold on to the good memories and purge the bad."

"Where does Jackson fit in?" Lacey asked.

"He's a gray area," Lila said. "So he'll have to go."

They dipped their heads and watched her turn toward the exit. Lila heard their voices behind her.

"That Brody really did a number on her," Regina was saying. "I've never met someone so untrusting in all my life."

"That's rich, coming from you," said Pascalle.

"What?" Regina demanded. "You think I'm untrusting just because I like to make sure people are the real deal before I open up to them? Making mistakes in relationships can get you burned."

"I suspect that's just what Lila's thinking," Lacey said.

"I hope Jackson *buries* that Brody jerk," Regina said.

Chapter Twenty-one

A crowd of well-wishers, mostly staff members but also a few guests, lined the shore, cheering Jackson's name while Brody sulked.

"I can't concentrate with this racket. It's not fair if they don't shut up so I can focus," Brody said.

Jackson narrowed his eyes at him, wondering what Lila might have once seen there. "Just some friends showing support."

Brody scanned the crowd, still frowning; then his eyes lit up. "Lila's not here. Guess she didn't want to offer you support. I bet she's shaken up from seeing me, or trying to think up ways to beg me back."

"You keep telling yourself that, *buddy*." Jackson slipped his hands into his water-ski gloves.

Brody went for the jugular. "When I saw her the other day, she told me she was grateful to see me. Said she'd been hoping I'd come after her, because she couldn't stand all these cowards who hide away here in fantasyland, too afraid to face the real world."

Jackson laughed. "Like you hide out at school biding time so you don't have to get a real job?"

Brody sneered at him. "At least I'm not some beach bum waiting to grow old so the state can support me. At least I have an education."

Jackson laughed again. If Brody was trying to hook him, he was using the wrong bait. Jackson wondered if other people thought he was here because he had no better prospects, but then he brushed off the notion. He didn't care what other people thought.

Jackson eased to a seated position on the pier to don his skis.

Brody cast an exaggerated look over a group of teenage girls at the shoreline. Flexing his arms, he dipped his body over the edge of the pier into the water. When he pulled himself back up a few seconds later, his face was red. "Cripes. That's freezing!" Water streamed off the surface of his neoprene wetsuit vest and black ski shorts. The girls giggled.

"The water's at least seventy-two degrees," Jackson said.

"My blood's thinner than yours."

Jackson didn't bother to respond. He peeled his faded T-shirt over his head, leaving him in just the skis, water-ski gloves, and swim trunks. The group of girls near the pier sucked in their breath before he shrugged into a standard-issue life vest.

Brody eyed him. "It's going to be a timed race?"

"Yep."

"You already know the lay of the water. I think I should have a handicap if this is going to be a fair race. And I think I should choose the timekeeper."

Jackson shrugged. "Suit yourself. Would it be enough of a handicap for you if I ski slalom?"

Brody laughed. "Nice try, waterboy, but you can't trick me. I've heard some slalom racers are faster than on two skis. To make this a fair race, you'll have to . . ." He rubbed his chin for a second as he savored laying down the rules. "You'd have to ski *barefoot.*"

Jackson raised his eyebrows. "You think that'd be fair?"

"No doubt you know this course like the back of your hand. Barefoot's the only fair way."

"Suit yourself," Jackson said again, kicking off his skis. "No excuses and no rematches. Agreed?"

"Agreed."

"Who's your timekeeper?" Jackson asked.

Brody's lips stretched wide over his teeth as he watched a woman step from the crowd. "Jenna."

Jenna climbed up to the pier to the end, where she took the stopwatch from Brody and gave Jackson a coy smile. "Ready, boys? You've got quite a crowd today."

Brody wrapped an arm around her. "Keep good time for me, sweetheart."

Jenna cast him a withering look and ducked out from under his arm. "Just get out there and ski. You're up first." She blew a whistle to draw the crowd's attention. This wasn't a resort-sponsored event, so Tustin wasn't present to announce anything. If it hadn't been for Jenna's whistle, the start of the race would have been as unceremonious as Brody dipping back into the water and grabbing the rope. The boat's engine roared, and all eyes went to the pale-haired man in the water.

Jackson had to admit that Brody surprised him by having some skill as a skier. He hadn't exaggerated when he'd said skiing was his sport. On top of every curve, Brody even took the last jump with a spin, landing flawlessly. He swooshed across the finish line in just under four minutes.

Jackson held out a hand to congratulate him on the nice run, but Brody marched past, scanning the crowd. People who'd snubbed him earlier patted him on the back now. Even Jenna looked somewhat impressed.

"Told you skiing was my sport. Even so, I can't wait to play a little tonsil hockey with Lila," Brody called back over his shoulder with arrogant self-assuredness.

Jackson set his face in grim concentration, ignoring the

temptation to pick up the skis that Brody had dropped on deck and wrap them around his neck.

"Your turn, waterboy," Brody added with a cocky wink.

Jackson slid into the water, feeling its coolness rush between the vest and his bare chest. He signaled the driver, and the boat took off. Jackson leapt to his feet in its wake. He followed as the speedboat tore through the curves. He spun his head in the direction of the pier on the second turn and saw Brody looking at the stopwatch, frowning. Jackson knew he had a good thirty seconds on Brody already, and he planned to make it more. The crowd cheered. Jackson waved and spun in the air, then hunkered down, aiming for the fiberglass ramp. As he gained on the ramp, a hush fell over the crowd. Jackson hit the ramp full speed. His body propelled in an arch almost ninety feet through the air, plunging into the water at the other end. In three counts, he was back on his feet. He whipped his bangs from his eyes and sliced across the finish line, spouting a rooster tail.

Jackson hauled himself onto the pier and strode over to Jenna and Brody, shaking his hair to give Brody a dousing. "What's my time, Jen?" he asked.

Jenna frowned at the watch. "You got it soaking wet. It might be broken. I—"

A joyful scream pierced the air. Jackson turned to find Pascalle peering over Jenna's other shoulder. "Three minutes, forty seconds! Jackson won!"

The crowd responded with a roar. A throng of people pushed against Jackson, slapping his back and ruffling his damp hair. Brody inched his way through the crowd, sulking.

Jackson called after him. "Next time check the facts before you lay down the rules. The boat has to travel faster to keep a barefoot skier afloat. You pretty much negotiated yourself into a losing race."

Brody's face turned red behind his reflective glasses. "That's cheating. We should run the race again on skis."

"No rematches. Not that I wouldn't enjoy fleecing you on any number of skis."

"Jackson," Regina's voice called over the crowd. "A word?"

Jackson gave Brody a patronizing pat on the back before slipping through the masses to Regina. Her face was serious against the backdrop of celebrating onlookers. "What's up?" he asked.

"Tustin just called Lila into his office after taking a phone call from Scottsdale. I don't know what's going on, but I'm pretty sure you won't like it."

A sobering unease stabbed through Jackson. He couldn't risk losing Lila before he had a chance to tell her his news about why he'd left and the decision he'd made about expanding his business. Heck, he hadn't even had a chance to *tell* her about the business yet. He was still holding out hope she might consider going with him to get the new location up and running. He ran his hand through his hair as he thought of what he'd do if she said no. It wasn't an option he could face. He'd have to convince her to stay with him, but first, he'd have to get her to talk to him. "Thanks, Regina. I owe you one."

"No problem. Hey—nice job pummeling the moron."

As if summoned, Brody started by as someone else in the crowd caught Jackson's eye. He reached out to steer Jules by the elbow, then grabbed Brody with his other hand. He pulled the two together.

"Brody, meet your new boss. Jules, Brody. I suggest you start him out with diaper duty."

Lila closed the door to Tustin's office behind her. She'd gotten her way, but now she'd have to pay the price with her heart. Already half-dazed, she walked straight into a damp wall of muscle. She looked up to find Jackson's fiery eyes probing hers. Before she could duck around him, he clamped his hands on her shoulders and held her in place. She'd known he'd catch up with her sooner or later, but the timing couldn't have been worse. She was an emotional wreck. She let her eyes slide back up to his and was surprised to find that he looked both furious and worried. He'd probably have a few choice words for her, along with plenty of questions. She should have expected as much.

She hadn't expected that he'd save the interrogation for later. She barely had time to inhale before he lowered his lips to hers and her world became a flash of darkness focused around one tender point of light. Jackson slid his hands down her sides, pinning her against the door. Fever surged through Lila. Too stunned to fight him, Lila moved in response. She trailed her fingers over Jackson's skin, savoring the lean muscles of his damp chest. *Damp chest. The competition.* Her body went rigid and she clamped her lips shut.

"Lila," she heard Jackson whisper, but he seemed more shaken by their kiss than upset that she'd drawn back. "I missed you so much."

Lila felt a pang of guilt as she tried to slide her hand between them, creating a barrier. "I . . . I can't do this."

He dipped his head and brushed his lips across the sensitive spot on her neck, just below her ear. "Please don't ever shut me out again."

Lila's resolve wavered as she savored his hot breath against her neck. She dug her fingernails into the palms of her hands and forced herself to twist away. "No. I can't do *this*." She waved her hand between them. "You and me. *Us*. I can't do it."

Her words hit their mark. Jackson took a half step back to view her better, eyes searching. "Regina said you spoke with Tustin about something. Tell me you aren't leaving."

Lila straightened her spine and tried not to be mesmerized by his charm. "It's arranged. I'm flying home the Monday after the holiday."

Jackson's face went white. "Next weekend?"

Lila nodded, a lump clogging her throat. *I won't cry. I won't let him see one sign of doubt to latch on to and convince me to stay.*

"We should talk about this."

The lump dissolved and pent-up anger flared. "What? Like we talked about when you went traipsing off to God knows where?"

"I came back." Jackson's jaw was set in a stubborn line.

"I had no way of knowing you would. All I knew is that you were here one day and gone the next."

Jackson's eyes raked her face and softened. He reached out for her hand. She drew back.

"Lila, you didn't think for a second I'd use you? You know how I feel. There wasn't time to talk to you before I left, but I do want to talk with you now, more than anything. Well, almost anything." A wolfish grin crossed his features, and then he became serious again. "Lila. I tried, but there wasn't time."

"You didn't try very hard."

"I left a note."

Lila harrumphed. "Some note." Jackson seemed perplexed by that. He opened his mouth again, but Lila cut him off. "There wasn't time for this either. I had to make a decision or risk losing the chance to get my old job back."

"Is that such a bad thing, Lila? What if you didn't go back? Maybe there are better opportunities that you'll never know about if you don't open up to them."

Lila knew the look on her face must have been something akin to thunderstruck. Not go back? But that had always been the plan: earn enough money for tuition, then finish out school and join the real world. "I have to go back."

Jackson's face fell. "You wouldn't even consider other options?"

"Like what? Traveling from resort to resort until one day I wake up middle-aged, without an education to fall back on, forced to wait tables at the Crab Shanty because I chose to whittle away my life playing house in fantasyland?"

Jackson blanched. "This feels pretty real to me. *You* feel real to me. What difference does it make where we live and what we're doing, as long as we're together? Is paradise so bad?"

Lila stared at him. She'd hoped he might give her some indication he wanted more from life than to earn minimum wage driving a boat for some hyped-up resort, but he made it sound like that's where he wanted to be. Only he wanted to do it with her at his side. Her shock subsided, and she softened a moment. If she were honest, she wouldn't care where they lived or what Jackson did either, if they could be together. But this wasn't the real world, and all fantasies gave way to reality eventually. The reality was that she didn't know if she could trust him. At least not with her heart.

Jackson stiffened and took a step back, as if he'd somehow already understood her thoughts. "Lila, please tell me you don't believe I broke into your room and stole your journal."

Lila heard herself gasp. How would he know anything about it if he hadn't . . . if he hadn't . . . she couldn't finish the thought.

"Ryan told me he found your journal on the Navigator with the money missing. You don't believe I'd betrayed you for a few hundred bucks—or any amount of money, for that matter?"

Lila felt her chest constrict until she could barely breathe. Shouldn't he be the one under scrutiny?

"Lila?"

As she looked into his eyes, her defenses melted. "No, I guess I don't believe you'd steal from me."

Jackson slipped her hand into his. "I'm glad for that, at least. Come talk with me in private. I have something I want to tell you. Then maybe you'll change your mind about leaving." His eyes shone with passion, but not the kind they'd felt earlier. He wanted to talk to her. Lila wanted to scream *yes* and throw her arms around him, but she remembered that even if Jackson hadn't stolen from her, he'd gone off with hardly a word, and then there was still the postcard.

A door opened down the hall, and Drew stepped out of the

PR office to fill a cup at the water cooler. He noticed them leaning against Tustin's door. "Jackson, my man. I've got an answer for you on that question you asked me earlier. I've got about a half hour to spare if you want to stop in now. Otherwise it'll have to wait until after spring break. I've got a ton of work to do to prep for it."

Jackson tore his eyes away from Lila. "Thanks. Let me just . . ."

Drew held up his hand to signify he understood and bowed back into his office.

"Promise me"—Jackson leaned in closer to Lila. *Too close*—"you won't do anything drastic until we get a chance to talk."

Lila shook her head. "I can't . . ."

Jackson closed his eyes as if focusing all his energy on something beyond his abilities. "You're killing me here, Lila. Why?"

"It's not the journal, or the money. I believe you wouldn't take those from me, but there's something else I can't overlook. It's Emmalee." She closed her eyes, wanting to cry or hide, mortified by her own jealousy. When she heard the shock in Jackson's voice, her eyes flew open.

"Emmalee? How and what do you know about Emmalee?"

His bewildered face told her everything she hoped not to see but needed to know. She wasn't going to give him a chance to lie to her, or worse, think up a lie to tell to Emmalee. She couldn't bear the thought of being the other woman.

She squirmed away from the door and dashed out of Jackson's reach before he'd recovered. She made the mistake of glancing back over her shoulder before she reached the path. Jackson stood transfixed, watching her storm away. A look of crushing grief spread across his face. Her heart spasmed. Maybe it was unfair to lay all the weight of this on him. She'd been a willing enough partner. She had to say something, but what? If she let him talk, he'd do what Brody did and try to explain it away. If Jackson was one-tenth as relentless about it as Brody had been, she knew she'd cave. She had to do something to put an end to it now. She paused and took a deep breath, bracing to tell Jackson a crippling lie.

"I'm sorry, Jackson. Learning about Emmalee was disturbing, but it's mostly an excuse. The truth is, seeing Brody changed things. I've decided to go back to him. It's Brody I love, not you. I just didn't know it until he came after me."

She turned to shield her eyes so he wouldn't see the lie there. She wasn't quick enough to avoid seeing Jackson's face twist in pain.

Chapter Twenty-two

IN THE WORST OF TIMES, SUMMON YOUR OPTIMISM;
THEN GET READY TO KICK YOUR OPPOSITION'S BUTT.
LUCKY NUMBERS: 2 4 5 13 22 8

The pain might have been worse if someone had harpooned his heart, but Jackson doubted it. In fact, it would have been a welcome distraction. He stood motionless in front of the hostess podium and watched Lila and Brody at breakfast. Lila's carry-on bag sat at her feet. She had managed to avoid Jackson all week. He'd thought about cornering her, making her admit the feelings between them had been real, but he knew she'd resent it. He was going to have to let her go.

He'd spent long days out on the water every chance he had, thinking it through from every angle. If she still cared for Brody, he didn't want to stand in the way of her happiness. He spent hours sailing, in tune with the wind and the waves, trying to forget his pain, but he knew it was something he'd just have to get used to, because it wasn't going away. His heart may be broken, but he still had responsibilities to deal with.

Jackson had been assigned to the departures schedule this week. Unless he walked out on Tustin, which his conscience wouldn't allow him to do, he'd be forced to watch the happy couple depart. He squinted back toward the table and wondered why Brody didn't have any baggage with him. He'd already seen Lila's other luggage at reception, but he didn't recall seeing Brody's red roller bag.

"Looking for a table, sweetie?" Sophie asked.

"No, thanks. I'll take something to go."

"This is so *wrong*," Sophie continued, as if picking up an earlier conversation.

Jackson just nodded. He knew what she meant. He just didn't want to talk about it. "Want to join me, Jackson?" a woman's voice asked from behind.

Jackson didn't have to turn to know who it was. "No thanks, Jenna."

She looped her arm through his anyway, ignoring a death stare from Sophie, and tugged him toward the buffet line.

"Jenna, I'm not in the mood. I've got departures to work in fifteen minutes anyway."

Jenna batted her eyelashes, thick with mascara. "You'd be amazed what can be accomplished in fifteen minutes, Jackson."

Jackson stopped walking. "I'm getting tired of warding you off twenty-four-seven, Jenna. I'm not interested. I never have been interested, and I never will be interested. I've got a nasty feeling you had more to do with what happened with me and Lila than you'll ever admit. That's enough to make me dislike you, if it were worth the effort. It's not." He unhooked her arm and walked away.

Sophie stopped him before he could leave the restaurant. "Jackson Koble, you're my new hero. That was *long* overdue."

"It was a cruddy thing to say," Jackson admitted.

"And yet, it was a thing of beauty. Look at her. She's like the Dark Witch in *That Wizard of Ours,* as cold as stone. She doesn't even look upset."

Jackson leaned against the podium and turned so that he could see Jenna from the corner of his eye. Sophie was right. She didn't look bothered. She'd already composed her features and had approached the table where Lila and Brody were seated. Twin teenagers sat to the left of Brody, giggling at something he said and flipping their hair over their shoulders. Brody waggled his eyebrows and leaned in with too much of his body.

Jackson's eyes skidded to Lila, and he almost allowed himself a smile. Rather than being hurt by Brody's behavior, she'd relaxed her posture some. He doubted it was a result of exercising any newfound trust in Brody. More likely, she just didn't care. For the first time in almost a week, Jackson's spirits buoyed. Maybe there was a slim hope after all. He'd have to be careful how he acted on it. Lila probably wouldn't give him much opportunity to explain things while they were still wrapped up in what she called a fantasy world. He thought of her last words to him. *I love Brody. I just didn't know it until he came after me.* After he forced the stab of pain away, he could think logically about it. He knew Lila well enough to know her affections didn't flow with the tides. He wasn't in one day and out the next because she'd changed her mind. She was just confused. Maybe, after she found some comfort in familiar surroundings, he'd be able to convince her that the feelings between them were real.

Jenna joined Lila at Brody's table. Lila barely glanced up. She picked at a croissant while Brody shoveled down hash browns. Jenna smiled at him and then leaned across the table, holding his jaw in her hand while she wiped away a strand of potato sticking to the corner of his lip. Brody straightened in his seat, and the teenagers slumped in their chairs. Lila didn't seem to care either way. She stood up to leave and told Brody to collect his bags from his room and meet her by reception.

Brody ran his eyes over her while leaning back in his chair. "You sure you don't want to go back to the room with me? It's a long flight."

Lila winced, but then her eyes flicked to him and Sophie, and she gave Brody a tight smile. "I want to say good-bye to a few people, but don't worry—it's a long cab ride too."

Brody leaned in to her for a kiss.

Something inside Jackson rumbled like a wild beast. He had to concentrate to keep from baring his teeth. Fortunately, Lila only trailed her fingers across Brody's cheek before turning away. Jackson let out a breath and turned to Sophie. "She'll probably want to say good-bye to you. I'll make myself scarce."

"Please don't tell me you're giving up, Jackson. We can't leave Lila to the worst shark of them all," Sophie pleaded.

"Sorry, Soph. It's what Lila thinks she needs, and I want to respect her wishes . . . at least for now." He winked, then took a step away. He turned back for a second. "Have you seen Ryan anywhere?"

"He and Lacey have Twilight tonight, so they've got the morning off. They're probably up on the roof for some privacy."

Jackson smiled. He was glad to hear Lacey and Ryan were still a couple. He'd offered Ryan a job helping set up the new business in Puerto Rico and working a tour boat. He hoped he'd be able to talk Lacey into joining them. She'd be great with the kids, and Jackson would need all the help he could get in the beginning. He only wished he'd been able to share his vision with Lila. Soon. He had to give her a little time to straighten out her thoughts, but soon.

Sensing Lila approach from behind, he turned and held her gaze for a few heartbeats. He infused the look with as much tenderness as he could muster, hoping to convey that *she* might be confused, but *he* knew they belonged together. He lifted his hand, caressing her cheek with his thumb, hoping she'd pick up on the contrast between the sincerity of his gesture and the one she'd just given Brody. Then he let his arm drop and jogged out the door.

Lila watched after Jackson, dazed. Sophie brought her back to the moment.

"Time to go already?" Sophie asked.

Lila lifted her hand to her cheek where the skin tingled as if burned. The urge to run after Jackson nearly overwhelmed her, but she forced herself to remember she wasn't the only woman in the picture. Ignoring instincts in favor of wishful thinking had burned her in the past. She didn't intend to walk into that trap again.

Then why are my instincts telling me something's different this time?

Lila ignored her inner voice and hugged Sophie, eyes watering. "Thank you for *everything,* Sophie. I'll never forget you. Keep in touch, and let me know where you and Emilio go after the season so I can write."

Sophie's eyes misted too. "We're staying on another season. Emilio's going to be sous chef, so we're not going anywhere for a while."

"Oh, Sophie, that's great!" Lila hugged her even tighter. "Congratulate him for me, and tell him good-bye. I'll miss you."

Sophie's face lit up. "Maybe if your fortunes are successful in New York, you can help us with some connections there. We're thinking that after another two more seasons here we might settle down and get married, try our luck in the big city."

I guess a pot of gold exists at the end of the rainbow for some people.

"That's wonderful, Sophie. I haven't heard from Joshua yet, but either way, I'm sure he'd be more than happy to help." Lila gave her a warm smile. She was going to miss Sophie.

Lila had already said good-bye to Pascalle and Regina, along with Patrick, Tustin, and a bunch of others. This wasn't the first time someone had confided in her their hopes for the future. It seemed everyone had ambitions related to their real-world passions waiting in the wings. Even those transferring to a sister resort for the next season envisioned being there a year or so maximum before returning to reality. She thought of Jackson and how content he seemed with resort life. Instead of resentment or disappointment, Lila felt a tug of longing. Living in a fantasy world with Jackson had felt good. She wished fairy tales could come true for real. Emmalee, whoever she was, probably felt the same way.

"Who's left to say good-bye to?" Sophie asked.

"Just Lacey and Jules. I'm heading over to Little Delights now. I have a half hour before my cab gets here."

"If you don't find Lacey at Little Delights, you might check the sunning roof. Last I heard, that's where she and Ryan were headed."

Lila watched Brody at the breakfast table, in seventh heaven with the attention of the girls. She was surprised Tustin had offered him a position working at the resort. She might have been flattered that Brody wanted to go home with her, but something told her it had more to do with not being able to handpick the water-ski job. Apparently, it was diaper duty or nothing for Brody.

She couldn't wait to ditch him the minute the cab left resort grounds.

It didn't take long to say good-bye to Jules, and since Sophie was right about Lacey not being at Little Delights, Lila veered toward the staff building to find her. She didn't relish the thought of interrupting Lacey and Ryan, but she couldn't leave without saying good-bye to them. She checked her watch. Ten more minutes and she'd need to be at the curb, or they'd risk missing their plane. She hoped Brody would be waiting for her. She didn't want to prolong the departure. Her resolve was partly cracked already.

Ryan and Lacey didn't hear the knock. When Lila opened the door to the sunroof she saw two bodies entwined on the rickety beach lounge. The man was whispering sweet nothings. Lila stiffened, a feeling of disgust creeping over her. Those whispers sounded familiar. She couldn't let this happen to someone she cared about.

"Lacey, *no!*" Lila burst through the door. "*He's not worth it. Ryan is so much more—*" Lila's words hung in the air as she stared down at the startled bodies in horror. She'd been right about the voice. Brody looked up with unfocused eyes. Lila looked down at his partner. *Jenna.*

* * *

"Cripes, Lila. What's the big deal anyway?" Brody clipped at Lila's heels toward reception.

Jackson stood near the bench outside at the curb with Lacey and Ryan. The three watched Brody and Lila with fascination. Jackson had to bite the inside of his lip to keep from whooping with joy. Then Lila's face came into view, and his joy morphed to fierce protectiveness. She wasn't physically or emotionally hurt, that much he could see, but she was furious. If Brody had tried to force himself on her, he was going to pay with a pound of flesh.

"It was one kiss," Brody complained.

Jackson felt Ryan's hand on his shoulder, willing him to wait and see how the scene played out. Neither Lila nor Brody realized they had an audience.

"That was more than one kiss—not that I give a rat's behind. I should have known you couldn't be trusted to act like you cared about me long enough to get me out of this place."

"You're overreacting, Lila. I do care about you. It's just that Jenna is so . . ."

Jackson couldn't believe the man was stupid enough to stand there confronted by Lila's rage and give her a goofy smile while thinking about some other woman. Lila's arm came back, fist clenched. Brody didn't see it coming. She jabbed him with a sharp right to the jaw. Jackson winced. That would hurt later. He just hoped she'd have the good sense to put ice on it so her knuckles wouldn't bruise.

Brody's knees folded under him. Before he even hit the floor, Lila stomped toward the waiting cab.

"What'd you do that for!? You know what, Lila? You're a prude. And you're not worth it."

Ryan tightened his grip on Jackson's shoulders.

"Any normal guy is going to look the other way once in a while. Jenna came on to me, and I'm not sorry she did. In fact, I like Jenna. I sure as heck like her better than you right now."

Lila spun, seething. "As far as I'm concerned, the two of you are a match made in heaven. You deserve each other."

She spun back around, looking for her luggage. Jackson felt Ryan release his shoulder.

"Dude, if she knew you saw all that, she'd be mortified."

"Yeah," Lacey said, toeing Lila's bags. "And she's going to find out real soon."

"Say no more," Jackson said. He gave Ryan a clap on the back before jetting into the garden, receding into the cover of date palms.

Chapter Twenty-three

Lila walked under the canopy of olive trees toward Tour Paradise's Scottsdale office. With every step, she wished she were walking back toward what she'd left behind. She couldn't believe Jackson hadn't turned out to say good-bye, but then, what had she expected? In no uncertain terms, she'd told him she loved another man and didn't want anything more to do with him. The part of her that hoped he'd see through her reckless lies died when she got on the plane in Fort Lauderdale. Alone.

She bristled at what Jackson would think when he learned Brody had stayed behind at the last minute to be with Jenna. She took a gulp of iced coffee and wished her flight hadn't gotten in quite so late or that Cliff hadn't wanted her into work quite so early. She entered the lobby, and the sobering atmosphere of reality hit her. She looked up the atrium at the third-floor railing, behind which the unseen world of Tour Paradise buzzed with activity. Sunlight strained to filter through the skylight in the ceiling, illuminating columns of floating dust. A pair of potted palms flanked the entrance, overwatered, leaves waxy. Lila pressed the elevator call button and waited while it descended from the top floor. She could've taken the stairs, but she didn't have the heart to face the dark staircase after having spent so

178

many pleasant weeks in the fresh salt air. Besides, if she remembered correctly, the staircase smelled like rubber tires.

Her mind flicked to the sweet ocean smell that always clung to Jackson. Her heart lurched in her chest. *What had she done?* Did she believe Jackson had been stringing her along? Even if someone back home pined for him, nothing in the postcard proved Jackson returned the sentiments. Maybe Emmalee was his eighty-year-old neighbor or an old schoolteacher. If she hadn't acted so stupidly, he'd have had the chance to tell her.

Her insides clenched. If she had given him the chance, she knew he would have told her the truth. Brody may prey on women with shaky self-confidence, but with Jackson, you got what you saw. No pretensions, no lies, no manipulation, just Jackson. And if he wasn't overly ambitious, and took one day at a time, well, maybe she could learn a thing or two from him. She'd always been so structured and inflexible. The moment things fell apart she focused on putting them back together, never stopping to ask if she'd end up with what she'd wanted. School was a necessity, but she'd never felt more free than when she'd gotten away for a while. Sure, she wanted to finish, but what was the hurry? And what did it matter where she lived? Florida had universities. Heck, every state in the United States had universities.

The elevator dinged, and the doors opened. Lila forced herself inside the stale carpeted box and rode to the third floor. Dozens of people milled about in Tour Paradise T-shirts, shorts, and flip-flops, downing lattes and chatting about their last vacation. Behind the glass doors leading to the call center, half the staff was already on the phones. Still, it was a few dozen people less than the last time she'd stood in this office.

The receptionist sent Lila straight back to Cliff and then went back to playing computer solitaire.

Cliff stood in front of his office, sipping an espresso. He

put it down when he saw Lila and opened his arms in a welcoming gesture. Lila gave him her best smile and kissed him on the cheeks.

"What is this?" Cliff said. "You look like you've come from a funeral."

"No, I'm great. I'm perfect. I'm glad to be here," Lila lied.

Cliff regarded her. "I'll take your word for it. You do look . . . changed. Working on locale can do that to a person. What doesn't kill you makes you stronger, right?"

"Unless it kills you," Lila said, making a note to capture something like that for Joshua. He'd want his next installment of fortunes soon, and she'd been too depressed to write anything this past week. She had some catching up to do.

Cliff rubbed his hands together. "Right. So, you ready to start these interviews? I'll give you a rundown of the characteristics we're looking for. You'll be hiring mostly for the Mexico location, but there are a few positions in Encantadora to fill."

Lila's interest was piqued. "Really, who's leaving?"

"Just your standard end-of-season turnover. I'll bring you the file later. Mexico first. Let's go over the questions and the ranking system. Your first interview is"—he looked at his watch—"in a half hour, and it's pretty much back-to-back from there."

Lila tried not to grimace. It wasn't Cliff's fault she was second-guessing her decision to leave Encantadora so soon and not stay on another season with Jackson. She was the one who'd asked to come back; she might as well make herself useful. "The busier you keep me, the better," she said. "I appreciate everything you did to bring me back. You won't regret it."

Cliff rubbed his chin. "You're welcome, but I want to be clear. I've got work for you now, but until we have a real turnaround in sales, this is sort of a no-strings-attached deal on both sides. Can you live with that?"

Lila surprised herself by how she handled those words. They didn't throw her into a panic. It wasn't that she didn't *care*. It was just that it didn't matter quite as much anymore. She knew she would be okay no matter what happened. "I understand, and I'm ready to jump in while you need me."

Cliff smiled at her. "You really have changed, Lila."

After seven interviews, including ones with two egomaniacs and a girl who squealed every answer, Lila had only one person earmarked for a second interview. Cliff assured her they'd all mastered the skills, or they wouldn't have made it past the initial screening, but it took a special person to relate to others in a way that fostered confidence and inspired trust. She knew a little bit about that now. Tomorrow she'd have to lower her expectations, or no one would come close to meeting her standards.

Cliff poked his head through the crack in the door. "Ready for one more?"

Lila looked up from her stack of assessments. "I don't have anyone else on the list."

"A last-minute write-in. Water-ski instructor."

Lila bent over the paper in front of her to finish scoring the last one and waved her hand. "Send him in."

She heard the door close, then open. "I'll be right with you." Lila checked the rank-order boxes like Cliff had shown her. She decided to send the last one on for the second interview after all. If the water-ski instructor wasn't too bad, she could call it three and go home without too much guilt.

She felt the presence behind her before she saw the arm reach around to set a fortune cookie onto her notepad. Heat radiated off the body behind her. She stared at the cookie, and her heart spluttered. She cracked it in half, spilling the shards into her lap. The words on the narrow strip of white were difficult to read through the tears. A familiar voice from behind read them with tenderness: SOMEONE WHO LOVES YOU OFFERS YOU THE DREAM OF A LIFETIME. SAY YES.

She turned, afraid the image she'd yearned for would disappear before she could latch on and hold it tight. When she saw Jackson, her heart nearly stopped. He loomed over her in faded jeans and a black polo, his lips curved into a careful smile, but anxiety dominated his eyes. He probably thought she'd push him away again. Lila's chest ached at the uncertainty in his expression. She wanted to wipe it away with a thousand kisses, but first she needed to let him know she'd made a terrible mistake. "Jackson—"

"Lila." Jackson's voice was full of agony. "I'm sorry, I—"

Lila closed her eyes tight and shook her head. "No, wait. I need to say something first." She swallowed hard. "*I'm* the one who should be sorry. I tried to ignore everything that was real between us and instead clung to petty suspicions. I pushed you away without letting you explain. I was wrong."

Jackson wiped a tear from her cheek with his thumb and then took her trembling hands in his palms. Lila's heart kicked up again. *He's going to forgive me.*

"It's not your fault, Lila. Pascalle explained about the postcard and the note. It was terrible timing—no doubt crafted by Jenna—but still, I understand how you must have felt. One minute we're loving each other, and the next I'm gone."

Lila thought she'd melt at the way he said *loving each other.* It conjured images of cool sand and time standing still. Jackson's furrowed brow told her he was tortured by the pain he thought she'd gone through. He locked eyes with her. Wildfire spread from her core to every extremity. She was surprised that the tips of her hair didn't burst into flames under his stare.

"You have to know I couldn't fake my feelings for you. I'm in love with you, Lila. *I love you.* I haven't said that to another human being in a long time, never to a woman other than my mom, and trust me, this is a whole different kind of love. Pug . . . Emmalee, is just a close friend from childhood. She's like a sister to me."

"A sister," Lila said. She'd gladly share Jackson with a sister figure if it meant getting him back.

"She just got married in Vegas. I sent the flowers to congratulate her. She knows all about you and wants to meet you." His beautiful eyes implored her to believe him.

Lila couldn't help it; she started to laugh. She'd been ready to love him the minute she saw him, but the news about Emmalee left her weightless. "I believe you. I'm sorry I ever doubted you to begin with."

Jackson's face was wiped clear of worry. He bent in close, covering her mouth with his. She threw her arms around his neck and held him tight. She never wanted to let him go. Jackson wrapped his arms around her waist and returned the kiss with the same zeal, then tore away. Darn it, he was always tearing away just when it was getting good.

When he spoke again, his voice cracked with emotion. "Lila, come back with me."

"Back to Florida?" she asked, but she was already nodding. She'd follow him to the ends of the earth if he asked.

Jackson shook his head, lowering into a chair and urging her to take one. He turned it so they sat knee to knee and he held her hands in his, raising one to his lips and brushing them across her swollen knuckles.

"Were you hurt when you hit Brody?"

"You know about that? Brody's more annoying than anything. Is that why you don't want to go back to Florida? Because of Brody? I see from the files he decided to stay on to fill one of the Little Delights positions, after all."

"Brody does nothing to improve the place, but I wouldn't let him chase me away. No, I was hoping—" His eyes fell away, and his hand reached for his jeans pocket.

"Hoping what?" Lila held a hand flat against his cheek. There would be no more unspoken secrets. Open communication was going to be the main theme in the next chapter of her life. She was tired of skulking around with suspicions.

"I was hoping you might agree to come with me to Puerto Rico." Jackson looked up at her under dark blond lashes. He looked so vulnerable she wanted to throw her arms around him again. The only thing stopping her was the awkward way he fingered whatever was in his pocket. She forced herself to focus on his words.

"Puerto Rico? There's no Tour Paradise in Puerto Rico."

"That's true. I've been thinking of building my own little paradise there, but it wouldn't be complete without you. There's American University, where you can finish your degree."

Blood rushed through Lila's veins, flooding her heart. "I like the sound of that, but how would we live?" The minute the words were out, she cursed herself. *Why can't I enjoy a romantic moment without thinking about practical matters?*

Jackson grinned. "I never got a chance to tell you, Lila, but I didn't intend to stay in Florida long. I just needed to get away for a few months after my father died, until I was ready to face the world again."

Lila raised her other hand, cradling his face. "I'm so sorry."

Jackson removed his hand from his pocket and reached up to take both her hands in his again. "I thought getting away would make things less painful, but it felt worse to know I could be making a difference but instead chose to hide. I've made a decision now that I feel at peace about. My father and I had a boat tour business on an island off the coast of Savannah, Georgia. It's mine now, and I've decided to expand it. That was my father's dream. The reason I left for those few days was to check out a property in Puerto Rico. After seeing it, I think I can make a difference there."

"You own your own business?" Lila asked, feeling a little dazed. It was a successful business, by the sound of it. Businesses in trouble didn't bother with expansion.

Jackson nodded again. "I bought the property last week. It's going to be a lot of work, sort of a massive restoration project, but it'll be worth it. Lacey and Ryan are going to join me at the end of the season. I plan to give kayak tours in the mangroves, and Ryan will handle the ocean tours and deep sea fishing." He paused, searching her eyes. "I made the plans hoping I could convince you to go with me."

Lila wanted to shout for joy. Did she deserve to get everything she ever wanted in one day? Someone who loved her. Someone who needed her for herself.

Jackson's face had become anxious again as he waited for her answer. She decided not to keep him in misery. "I could use a little restoration myself." Lila smiled.

"To be honest, it needs a lot of restoration," he said with measure.

"So do I. I've been too inflexible with my plans, but that's about to change."

The creases on Jackson's forehead smoothed and he leaned forward to kiss her again, but pulled back at the last second. "There's one more thing." He reached into his pocket for a silk pouch. "I know we haven't known each other long, but I'm a bit of a traditionalist, being raised in the South and all." He looked at her with open affection. "You've already made me happier than I could've hoped, but there's one more thing I need . . ." He dropped off the chair and onto one knee. "Lila, you're the only woman I've ever loved. Say you'll marry me and make me the happiest man on land or water."

Lila stared unmoving at the object in Jackson's hand. He drew open the strings and slipped out a ring, holding it in front of her finger. The white gold setting was forged in the shape of a Cherokee rose, a single-carat diamond perched in the center. Tiny emerald flecks set into the band trailed like little vines around the edges.

"It was my mother's." Jackson's voice was gravelly.

Reality came at Lila in a rush. She held out her hand to let Jackson slip on the ring. She barely had time to say yes before he scooped her up and buried her cry of happiness with a kiss. He set her on her feet but left his lips on hers. They trailed down her neck and back up again.

"Ahem," a woman's voice interrupted.

Jackson slowly, almost painfully it seemed, pulled his lips away from Lila and turned to face the open door. The receptionist stood behind a small woman with spiky hair and a lanky man wearing a flannel shirt with cut-off sleeves. The receptionist gave Lila a speculative look that said she was more delighted than embarrassed at having caught her in the throes of passion with one of her interviewees.

Jackson introduced them. "Lila, I'd like you to meet Emmalee."

"Pug to you, missy," the woman said, grinning.

Jackson returned the smile. "And her *husband,* Fish. Pug, Fish, *this* is Lila Hayes." He wrapped an arm around Lila's shoulders. "You caught us in a moment of celebration. She just agreed to marry me."

Pug squealed. Fish shuffled his feet and pumped Jackson's hand.

The racket drew Cliff from his office. "What's going on here? I take it you decided to hire someone?"

"No, sir." Lila laughed and broke free of Pug's hug. "In fact, he's not qualified."

"Oh?" Cliff's brows shot up.

Jackson cocked an eyebrow at her. "I'm not?"

"Nope. In fact, that's a perpetual misunderstanding that has to end. This man is not a water-ski instructor."

Cliff crossed his arms in front of his chest. "Then what is he?"

Lila smiled. "He's a tour boat operator. And he's the man I plan to let float my boat for the rest of my life."